# Becca's
## Story

# Becca's Story

JAMES D. FORMAN

CHARLES SCRIBNER'S SONS · NEW YORK
Maxwell Macmillan Canada · Toronto
Maxwell Macmillan International
New York · Oxford · Singapore · Sydney

Charles Scribner's Sons Books for Young Readers
Macmillan Publishing Company
866 Third Avenue, New York, NY 10022

Maxwell Macmillan Canada, Inc.
1200 Eglinton Avenue East, Suite 200
Don Mills, Ontario M3C 3N1

Macmillan Publishing Company is part of
the Maxwell Communication Group of Companies.

First edition     10  9  8  7  6  5  4  3  2  1
Printed in the United States of America

Library of Congress Cataloging-in-Publication Data
Forman, James D.
    Becca's story / James D. Forman. — 1st ed.       p.      cm.
    Summary: A Civil War romance concerning a Michigan girl and the
two soldiers who are rivals for her hand.
    ISBN 0-684-19332-9
    1. United States—History—Civil War, 1861–1865—Juvenile fiction.
[1. United States—History—Civil War, 1861–1865—Fiction.]       I. Title.
PZ7.F76Be   1992     [Fic]—dc20       92-1375

*T*his book owes thanks to a great many people: first and foremost to my wife, Marcia, who painstakingly and with love transformed so many old letters into readable type. Without her efforts there would be no story. Then there was my grandfather, who preserved and passed along the family material, as did my father, together with their fascination with the Civil War, and my mother, who as a child knew these young people in their old age. Thanks particularly to Charlie, Becca, and Alex, whom I trust are tolerant of the liberties I have taken with their lives.

# Contents

# Becca's Story

# ONE

*Gypsy Fortune*

ON FEBRUARY 6, 1859, fourteen-year-old Rebecca Frazer Case put pen to paper and wrote: "I am about to commence a daily journal, but how long I will keep it up I cannot say." She would in fact persist for a good many years, dutifully recording school, social, and church events, daily chores, weddings, and funerals.

Nothing at all remarkable was reported until October 24, 1860, a day which began with the kind of terror never encountered in Becca's most disturbing dreams. It ended with the exciting, yet uneasy, conviction that her childhood was finished.

The sun was announced, as usual, by the rooster's first strident crows. Instinctively, Becca pulled the quilt over her head. Then, remembering it was a red-letter day, Jonesville's annual Harvest Festival, she sat up in the dawn's clear golden light. Fair weather meant she could wear the new calico dress: two-dollars-and-fifty-cents' worth of fabric from Brower's store and two weeks of Ma's tedious sewing, since Pa had not yet set aside money for one of the new sewing machines. All would be worth it for the annual picnic and the ball at the Waverly House, to which Becca would be escorted by not one but two beaux. Nowhere amid such happy anticipations did she foresee the strangeness of the morning that lay ahead.

Becca did not panic easily. She fancied herself a self-possessed urban girl, quite smart and mature for fifteen years, and the mirror above the washstand, in support of this appraisal, threw back the image of a slim, almost sharp-featured, but very pretty girl. She would never be one of the "stunners" the boys ogled in *Harper's Weekly*—"indecently lush," her mother called them—but there were no such stunners in Jonesville. In photographs Becca's delicate loveliness took on an air of apprehension, as though she expected the camera to explode. In fact, however, Becca could calmly manage a wild horse, happily sing before a large audience of strangers, and undoubtedly would have survived one of the Indian assaults that now belonged only to southern-Michigan folklore.

Her hair had never yet been cut. Of late, however, Ma had begun calling hair worn long and loose unladylike and threatened to get out the sheep shears if Becca would not put her hair up. Since this would disclose her one physical embarrassment, enormous ears, Becca resisted scraping her hair to the top of her head. Nor did she want to hack off her tresses as Liddie had done, even though "bobbing" was the latest fashion.

The wafting aroma of frying pork chops pulled Becca from her reverie, drew her downstairs, across the hard-packed yard to the privy, then back to the washstand in the hall, with its china bowl of clear water. Only then did Becca join the others. Sarah Case, mother of seven, looked too fragile for the physical demands thrust upon a midwestern farm wife. Of her children, three were gone. Franklin, Jr., was married to Clara Baxter and off seeking his fortune. Sarah and Emma were married and living in New York. Douglas, too, was talking of marriage; he had already left to pick up his Julia for the festival. Younger than Becca was her brother Theodore. A whiner, Dora, as he was called, kept largely to himself amid a burgeoning colony of caged chipmunks in the barn. Becca's admitted favorite was the youngest, George, who already kept a diary and aimed to become a reporter for the *New York Herald*.

Absent, as usual, from the family circle was Pa, Franklin Benjamin Case, Sr. When he was in one of his eruptively volcanic moods, the household trembled, but as a rule Pa made Becca—and even Ma, who on principle disapproved of wasting energy on laughter—laugh a good deal. They all were accustomed to Pa's absences; life took on a more lulling rhythm when he was away. Should an unlikely grizzly bear break into the house, Ma would be there to admonish him with a Bible in her hand and would, if need be, die protecting her children. And Pa? Becca wasn't quite sure about Pa, the gentleman farmer, occasional innkeeper, and owner and trainer of celebrated trotting horses. He would probably avoid the need to shout down the bear, his black beard bristling with rage, by conveniently not being present. Yes, Becca had reservations about Pa. Should she ever face the obligation of choosing a spouse, she meant to keep her emotions under control and choose wisely.

With the dishes washed, the pigs and chickens fed, and the cow milked, Becca fetched horse and wagon from the barn. Dora and George were not going into town, and their mother admonished them to keep the house locked and to be wary of strangers. There were Gypsies in town. "I've heard tell they roast tasty boys like yourselves over their camp fires," she warned, not entirely in jest. But the Gypsies were not on Becca's mind as she and Ma set out for Jonesville under a clear blue sky. On either side of the rutted dirt road, trees still blazed with the fiery colors of an autumn that refused to die.

Go back two generations, and there would have been no road, no iron rails laid east and west, not a dwelling that could not be folded up and dragged behind a pony. Only the Potawatomi Indians would have been out hunting. It was their moccasined feet printing an ageless trail along what would become the Michigan Pike between Detroit and Chicago that spelled their own extinction. In time their trail became a wagon road, and in 1828 Benaiah Jones, his wife, Lois, and their five sons rolled west along it, to be nurtured through the first hard winters by Chief Baw Beese. Within two years, the village of Jonesville was plotted at the only ford for ten miles in either direction on the Saint Joseph River. For a decade Jonesville remained the seat of Hillsdale County. By 1831 Mr. Jones did a thriving business at his Fayette House hotel, as a trading center grew up around the Sibley sawmill on the river. A year later the town's first ball was held at Jones's Tavern, with George Dunham offering a lively, if repetitious, version of "Money Musk" on his fiddle. It was the only tune he knew.

Eighteen thirty-three brought the Bell House school, built of logs, as was most of Jonesville at this time. Charles Gregory, Sr., became the postmaster. Both the general store and gristmill were rising when Benaiah Jones, who had begun it all, moved west again to Texas with his son Croesus, where the father would die violently for his Union sympathies.

Meanwhile, the Potawatomi, without whose assistance Jonesville would never have existed, were becoming obsolete, moving north, where the forests were still uncut, gone with the pioneers and the pelt hunters. Jonesville became a village of clerks and farmers.

4

Official religion came in 1835 when the United Presbyterians began to hold services in the session house, which they continued to do until they built their New England-style brick church nearly twenty years later. The turnpike was laid through town in 1837. By then there were a few graves in the cemetery on a little rise east of town. By the end of the 1840s a number of the early settlers had caught gold fever. Few of these self-styled Fayette Rovers returned from the gold fields of California, and none got rich. That same year, 1849, the Michigan, Southern, and Northern Independent Railroad deemed Jonesville important enough to make it a stop, and the depot was constructed. Two years after the formation of Jonesville's first fire company in 1856, Becca Case and her family arrived from New York to take up farming outside of town.

The proximity of the growing and friendly village did not make living there any less lonely for Becca, who still referred to Brooklyn as "my native land." But it was a lot better than Pulaski, a tiny crossroads hamlet eleven miles northwest, where her brother Franklin, Jr., lived, and to which her father was threatening to move because, he maintained, the grass there was better for his horses. Should that happen, Becca would make plans to return to New York, and no mistake. For now she would settle for the festival and those few attractions Jonesville had to offer.

Neither Becca nor her mother took much interest in the rural aspects of the festival, such as ox pulling or the judging of livestock, pies, and jams. Becca would have enjoyed the trotting races, since Pa had horses entered, but Ma had said no to that. She had said maybe to the political speeches that night.

For weeks, Jonesville had been anticipating the visit of Cassius Marcellus Clay. The appearance of that fiery abolitionist, supporter of Abraham Lincoln, was being billed as the event that would place Jonesville firmly on the map. Pa deemed the upcoming presidential election the most significant since General Washington's acclamation. Had Becca been given a vote, she would have cast it for the Little Giant, Stephen Douglas, who was supported by northern Democrats. The southern arm of that party backed John Breckinridge, and with the Democrats so divided, Pa said the Republican, Abraham Lincoln, was bound to win by default. When that happened, "get clear of the tracks," was his assessment of the consequences. Becca didn't really care a fig about political rallies, but hearing Cassius Clay meant she could stay up late with her friends.

Clay and Lincoln bunting was draped over upper Chicago Street near the academy where Becca learned algebra and rhetoric when Ma didn't need her at home. Next were the first brick houses, just before the road widened so that wagons might turn around, then the depot, the river, bridged now, and finally Jonesville's commercial heart, including the Waverly House. This was James Forman's boardinghouse, where his son, Alex, Becca's beau, would be working until noon when the picnic closed things down. Near the opposite corner stood the post office, the first stop for Becca and her mother. Becca saw no sign of Charlie Gregory, her other beau, who clerked there full-time for his father since his twin brother had left town without a by-your-leave. Nor were there any letters for the Cases, even though sister Sarah had a baby overdue.

"I believe I'll have my fortune told," Becca announced suddenly.

"No such thing," Ma replied. "We'll have nothing to do with the likes of Gypsies. What we'll do is visit that phrenologist fellow."

6

"Phineas Sherman?" Becca had seen the advertisement in the *Jonesville Weekly Independent* for the renowned phrenologist and knew her mother had a taste for the mysterious, as long as it was respectable. She would not approve of Gypsy tarot cards or crystal balls, but the scientific measurement of the living skull was another matter.

Ma pulled the horse and wagon to the wooden curbing beyond the depot, where red-white-and-blue bunting and a freshly painted sign indicated that Professor Phineas Sherman, Phrenologist, was sharing space with Jonesville's daguerreotypist for the day. It was fifty cents for a reading, expensive, but Ma'd been saving up egg money.

A young Gypsy woman in a bedraggled red satin skirt and flowered shawl crossed the street, smiled at Becca, and stepped toward her. "A fat fortune for a thin coin," she offered, her accent making her words nearly incomprehensible. "Only five cents, *kiahli*, to see the future."

"None of that," Ma said, grabbing Becca's arm and hurrying her into the phrenologist's studio, where they removed their bonnets and solemnly submitted to the measuring of their skulls with calipers, measuring tapes, and probing fingers, then waited, hands folded, for their charts to be prepared.

Becca scanned the results with interest, intending to transcribe them into her diary at a later date: (1) not inquisitive, (2) loves fine things (she approved), (3) mirthful (Ma would disagree, but then Ma was never mirthful), (4) dislikes children (perhaps; Becca had not made up her mind about children), (5) unfailingly honest (this she accepted without question), (6) thinks little of the opposite sex (at which she exclaimed aloud, "Ha! How many girls have two escorts to the Harvest ball?"), (7) petulant (she wondered if this word was in the old Johnson's dictionary), and finally, (8) a selfish streak.

This last quite offended Becca. Her inclination was to tear

the reading into strips there and then, largely because she'd heard the same thing from her mother last washday when she'd complained of the caustic soap and hot water. In response her mother had said, "Becca, I hate to say this, but sometimes I suspect you haven't one iota of family feeling." Apart from blowing her nose, a surprising sound for so dainty an organ, Becca had endured this admonition in silence and made no comment now to Phineas Sherman, though she meant to tell her diary later that, when she headed east, she would have servants of her own. She would do no more laundry ever.

Becca carefully folded the phrenological chart into her pocket and thanked the professor for his efforts. Then, with bonnets retied, the two ladies ducked out into the dazzlingly sunlit streets of Jonesville. Sarah's next stop was the quilting contest, where she had a sample of her own work entered, but Becca said she needed a sarsaparilla and would join her mother presently. This was not pure deceit. She was thirsty, and had crossed the street to the vendor's stand when a voice called out, *"Kiahli!"* It was the woman she had seen before, her red skirt all powdered with the dust of summer's endless road. "A fat fortune for a thin coin," the woman offered again. "Come, come," she said, beckoning toward a tent of dark-brown canvas.

The Gypsy put her arm around Becca's shoulder as they entered, a familiarity Becca did not, oddly, find disturbing. "Come, *kiahli,*" the woman urged gently, "come inside, little one."

A single candle on a table showed three stools and what Becca would recall as a very old child with an enormous head. Beneath the domed brow, the small face was the color of pale rawhide, as though a baking sun had shrunk the flesh to the skull. The eyes looked very sane, yet entirely mad at the same

8

time. "Our first client of the day," said the Gypsy woman to the child. "You must choose the cards well for this *kiahli*," at which the child's mouth parted in a grimace that might have been amusement. "*Kiahli* means 'little thin one' in our tongue," the woman explained, "and this is my son. A strange boy, with strange gifts."

Once all three were sitting about the small table with its guttering candle stub, the child's hands scrabbled through a deck of tarot cards with surprising speed and dexterity. The boy's scalding eyes remained fixed on Becca's as his thin, leathery fingers stirred, arranged, and rearranged the worn deck. Without glancing at the pack from which he dealt, the child laid out a cross-shaped pattern of nine cards.

"Here in the center is yourself, *kiahli*, the two of swords," explained the woman. Becca saw a female figure blindfolded, crossed swords in her hands, an empty sea with a crescent moon above. "Next, the present and the soon to be." These lay beneath the center card. First was the three of cups, three robed, dancing figures holding golden cups aloft. Then the six of wands, a mounted figure surrounded by men with clubs. "A good life thus far, *kiahli*, but you must beware of strife. Now the choices, *kiahli*. One always faces choices. Two cards to the left, two on the right." The woman laughed. "Behold the fool," she exclaimed, and Becca saw a wandering figure stepping blithely off the edge of a seemingly empty void. "Perhaps there is something of the Gypsy in you, *kiahli*? Now the eight of cups, the wanderer's card. Lonely, maybe, but not so bad. One could do worse. While on the other hand. . . ."

With this prompting, the child dealt the six of swords, a man poling a boat in which two hooded figures rode toward a far shore. Next, the six of cups, showing children in a flower garden. "The cards speak for themselves, do they not? A sad, uncertain journey, *kiahli*, followed by repose of spirit. And finally, the near and certain future." Her words encouraged her deformed son to shuffle what remained of the deck. He paused, still staring at Becca, his eyes glittering. Does he loathe me because I'm normal? she wondered. A grin of malignant delight seemed to illuminate his drawn face as he laid faceup the ten of swords, each weapon thrust deeply into the back of a prone man.

Becca must have shown alarm, for, with a conductor's flourish, the child laid down the final card, a black figure in armor on a white horse. Beneath the picture was emblazoned "Death."

"So end all stories," said the Gypsy woman as the child gathered up the cards.

Becca gripped the edge of the table, then withdrew her hands into her lap lest her fingers be seen to tremble. How foolish to be so horribly afraid.

"This need not be you," the Gypsy consoled, but the wavering, candlelit gloom and the triumph in the strange child's face sent waves of terror through Becca's body.

"I know they are only cards," Becca said very clearly, too clearly.

"Death," whispered the deformed child. He had not previously said a word. "Death," he repeated, and Becca felt the rootlet of every hair on her head. Death was her grandmother laid out on her bed in New York like a shrunken effigy of a vulture, smelling of lavender, her old stories of city life forever stilled, no more to urge Rebecca to be a good little girl. Death was a baby sister staring blankly out of her cradle one morning, never again to be a source of jealousy to Rebecca. Death was glimpsing Pa next day out by the woodpile, smashing the cradle to bits with an ax. Death was hearing him cry. Death had come to Becca's school last year and sat in the seat beside her. Death was cold and still and frightening. Death was forever.

"Death," recited the child once more, seeming to rise from his stool. Becca half rose herself, wanting the sunlight and people, her mother most of all.

By now the child had risen over the candle, his features probed by its wandering light, and, quite tenderly, the slim fingers of his hands moved to caress her hair, shaping the outline of her skull rather as the phrenologist had done, yet with considerable gentleness and a shy innocence and solicitude. "Yes, I am death," he whispered, the words spoken or only imagined—Becca was never quite certain. She had paid the fee. Now she was going to leave.

"For another thin dime I can tell you more," the Gypsy woman said, seizing her wrist. For an instant Becca froze, like a rabbit that sucks its flanks in and out with panic, yet is unable to move. Then she burst through the dirty canvas barrier into the splintering sunlight. "Come back!" The Gypsy's voice had a sharp edge. Dirty children played beside the brightly painted carts until they saw Becca, then ran to surround her and pluck at her skirts. In a panic, she brushed their hands away, ran, heard laughter follow her. Round about, smoke rose from dingy tents. Dark, shaggy-haired children seemed to drink her in with immense, luminous eyes. Becca felt trapped, though no one touched her or blocked her way, until, out of breath and panting, she could call out, "Oh, Ma!"

Only then, among the exhibition stalls, surrounded by the everyday, hard-working citizens of Jonesville, did she feel secure. "Oh, Ma, that was awful." Becca confessed her visit to the Gypsies, and she was clearly too upset for Sarah to remonstrate or even offer a gloating I-told-you-so.

"They say the same thing to everyone," her mother explained as they started for home. "Just put it out of your mind." But all along the road, Becca had the feeling they were being overtaken by something stealthy that grew steadily larger while she and the wagon diminished. Of course, when she looked over her shoulder, the road was empty, and before they reached the farm she was becoming angry. How dare they frighten a paying customer?

As they were stabling the horses, her concern must have shown, for Sarah said, "Honestly, Rebecca, it's over. It's time to freshen up and make yourself pretty for the picnic. Alex and Charlie'll be here in no time."

"Yes, Ma," Becca agreed, yet the anxiety lingered as she changed into the new calico dress and combed her hair. That morning remained a dark spider, webbed at the center of her life, an event that would rise in memory to be endlessly pondered.

# TWO

## *Alex and Charlie*

CUMULUS CLOUDS PILED UP OVER JONESVILLE on that Indian-summer afternoon, and under that devouring sky the wagon appeared minuscule as it boiled from town. Dust fumed up from the iron-shod wheels; it would be another seventy years before the valley road was paved. Two young men sat on the wagon box. At Ma's prompting, Becca had already invited Alex to the festival—after all, it was leap year—when a letter had arrived:

> Bec,
>
> I should be very happy of your company at the Harvest Festival. Please answer by return mail.
>
> C. W. Gregory

"My, such a popular girl," her mother had said. "That Gregory boy's a scamp. You'll have some decisions to make by and by. Just try not to hurt anybody, and that includes Rebecca Case as well." This time Becca passed her dilemma along to the boys, and, being best friends, they had decided as good friends should. Both would escort her to the picnic and to the evening ball, when Rohrig's Quadrille Band would hold forth at the Waverly House until midnight, unless the politicking drew off the crowd entirely. As far as Becca was concerned the music could go on until dawn. Though she might sympathize with one candidate or the other, she could never vote, and if politics were part of the man's world, with her light, quick step and trim figure, the ballroom was very much her domain.

As the wagon drew nearer, Becca could see that Alex Forman held the reins; it was, after all, his father's wagon, used to haul goods to and from the Forman general store. Once out of school, Alex expected to clerk there full-time, or possibly for the Gardiners, who operated the Jonesville woolen mill and an increasing number of general stores on the frontier.

Alexander Aberdeen Forman was the taller of the two boys and looked older, though both were seventeen. His eyebrows had filled out and there was a new hard slimness to his body. He looked already more man than boy, and a serious one at that. His dark-brown hair was brushed smoothly across his forehead like that of a child posed for a daguerreotype. With Becca and Charlie, he attended the Fayette Union School. He was a good student in Greek and Latin and a near-champion speller, having stood up to the end in last spring's spelling bee. Another year, and Alex would be off to Hillsdale College.

Clearly bright and scrubbed clean through, Alex never evaded things, but always confronted life head-on. He was itching to try his strength on the world, and if Becca found any fault, it was with his solemn purpose. "Learn to laugh more, Alex," she had urged him once. "Laugh at me, at anything. It would do you a world of good."

"What a foolish boy he is," she had confided to her diary,

about ready to give up on her devoted friend, but Ma wouldn't let her, and Ma was usually right. She entirely approved of Alex's sober demeanor and his protective attitude toward her daughter.

Charlie Gregory was another matter. His twin brother, Ephraim, had vanished last spring, bent on California gold. Becca had not known him well, but he and Charlie were clearly cut from the same tree. Some older folks said that even their mother couldn't tell them apart. Mostly it was the jaunty walk, as if there were springs in the heels of their shoes and each step was going to be a long one, if not one in complete defiance of the laws of gravity. They had the same expressive eyes lit by youth, curiosity, and the possibility of devilry, not to mention the notorious Gregory grin. But when the Gregorys were downcast, they were really down. "That Ephraim was hell-bent," Becca had heard more than once. Charlie had confided to Becca that he could not picture himself growing old. "Can't imagine myself huddling around the stove telling ancient stories," he said. "Can't happen, just can't."

"I like that boy despite himself," Becca's mother had said of Charlie Gregory. "But he's a rapscallion just the same," and she smiled as if recalling something long ago.

Hadn't the Sibley girl vanished from Jonesville precisely when Ephraim had headed west? Though neither had been seen since, both were discussed. Not gone west but gone bad, was Jonesville's verdict, yet Becca wished she'd known the Sibley girl. Had Ephraim made her nervous and excited, yet ready to giggle, all at the same time, the way Charlie sometimes made her feel?

Charlie liked to say that westering was in his blood, that he wasn't meant for clerking in the post office or farming. Wandering was the life. "Maybe you're a Gypsy foundling," Becca had said in jest. "Could be, Bec. One day, you'll see."

Roads called to him—morning roads, evening roads, north, south, east, or west, particularly west. He was simply in love with untraveled roads, unfollowed as yet, save in his dreams.

This venturing into the unknown excited Becca, but worried her. Respectable girls didn't do such things and, after all, her own dream was clear: east, back to New York.

"But seriously, Charlie," she'd persisted, "where will you go? I mean, in the end. There must be a special place."

At this he'd shrugged. "Not here. Maybe no special place." What mattered was the looking, the surprise beyond the next hill. No wonder the solid citizens of Jonesville, who had worked so hard to turn the wilderness into a safe haven, shook their heads over the Gregory boys, even though the boys had looked mild as milk working with their father at the post office, and it was grudgingly admitted that they were hard workers.

"Don't you mind folks talking?" she had asked him.

"I reckon it's a kind of compliment. I mean, deep down I expect they're jealous." Becca suspected Charlie might be right. She thought whoever talked about Rebecca Case would say, "What a nice proper girl; her mother must be proud."

Some nights Becca lay awake in bed, hearing the wild geese high overhead. Then she yearned for wings. She recalled her sister Emma reading aloud a book about a boy who ran away to sea, and she had asked, "But where do girls run away to?" Emma had replied with gentle irony, "Why, respectable girls excuse themselves quietly, then go up to their rooms and cry."

Once Charlie had said, "When the time comes, Bec, you ought to join me."

"Join you?"

"Going west, the two of us."

"Run off to those ridiculous mountains?" she'd scoffed, yet

was more disconcerted than she cared to admit. "Honestly, Charlie, I'm not that Sibley girl."

"Just think about it, Bec," Charlie had gone on. "I wish you were my sister. I'd teach you some confidence in yourself." His voice was friendly and coaxing, hard to resist, yet behind the ease was an electric tension, a devil-may-care attitude that worried her. And Charlie misread her entirely if he thought she was akin to the weathered women walking behind the covered wagons, or the sort with painted faces and feathered hats who waved from the westbound trains. "Soiled doves," Ma had called them.

Yes, Charlie made her restless.

She had put on her bonnet and was standing by the gate, ready, when the wagon pulled to a halt, and Alex, ever the gentleman, helped her with the picnic basket and handed her up to the wagon box. Charlie made room for her and grinned.

Alex tickled the flank of the old bay horse with the tip of the plaited buggy whip so that the grayish summer-shorn flanks flexed like fists, and they were off into the last glow of Indian summer, with all heaven's blue streaming overhead, so clear and warm that the day seemed to sing a chorus of content.

As the wagon rattled along, Becca thought with delight that she loved the day, loved both her escorts, was ravenously hungry, and wanted to sing. So as they went, they practiced for the upcoming holiday concert to be held for the benefit of troubled Kansas. Becca took the soprano, Charlie the tenor, Alex the bass, as they would at the Waverly House, as they had at the Templars' musical production of *William Tell*, which had played for three nights to a full house, with Alex as a youthful Tell and Charlie as his somewhat overgrown son. "Let's try 'Jeanie with the Light Brown Hair,' " Alex suggested, and the three harmonized, Charlie changing the girl's name to *Becca* on that jog-along ride to Thompson's Wood. There was a spontaneous, guileless joy about them, so rare among three friends, where there is always apt to be jealousy. Long before they reached the wood, they caught one another's eyes and dissolved into helpless, harmony-destroying laughter.

They passed the train tracks that led into town and stopped singing at the wail of the passing cars. Charlie stood up in the lurching wagon and waved both arms.

"Sit down; you'll break your neck," Alex warned him.

"Charlie, do be sensible," Becca agreed, but he waved until the train was out of sight.

"I wonder if that's the train Cassius Clay is on," Alex conjectured. "They say he's a great speaker." Clay of Kentucky was touring the west for Honest Abe Lincoln. In Coldwater, Michigan, a contingent of local Wide-Awakes had joined him to stir up the crowd. A torchlight parade was planned for Jonesville to conclude with fireworks outside the town hall.

"Clay's a great man," Charlie amended with surprising vehemence.

"A pistol-packing abolitionist, that's what," Alex emphasized.

"Oh, he'll have old Jonesville jumping," Charlie insisted, "and I don't mean to miss it."

"Nor I," Alex said seriously.

"Admit it," Becca said, "what you two don't want to miss is the fireworks."

"Clay's a great man," Charlie repeated, then broke into a face-dividing grin. "But if you'll excuse my language, damn right it's the fireworks."

Smiling broadly, Alex agreed.

"You two," Becca said, enjoying Alex's rare smile. "Mind-

18

less noise. Why do boys always love it so?" But she had to admit she was looking forward to the evening-ending display as well.

Jonesville's most outlying house on the route to Thompson's Wood was known as the Quaker farm, now abandoned and suspected of being haunted. No sounds of life issued from its long front porch, save the high-pitched "cheer, cheer, cheer" of the year's last crickets. The shabby house slumbered within its deep shadows, as still and cool as the halls of death, which made Becca's glimpse of an old man leaning on a long stick all the more startling.

"Look!" she said, but when the boys obeyed, the porch was one long shadow. When she described what had prompted her to cry out, Charlie asked, "Did he have a beard?"

"He might have," she answered, uncertain. "I think maybe, yes."

"Then perhaps it was old John Brown," Charlie said. Such fancies always seemed to kindle his imagination.

"John Brown's been dead and gone the best part of a year," Alex reminded him.

"Exactly," Charlie said with satisfaction. "But he spent the night there once." According to Charlie, the Quakers had helped slaves escape, and their farm was a regular stop on the abolitionists' underground railway to Canada.

"I'd heard that," Alex admitted.

But there was more. One night, Charlie said, the Quakers had housed John Brown and a band of escaping slaves from Missouri.

"Who says?" Becca asked skeptically. She might have been hazy on Cassius Clay of Kentucky, but everyone knew about John Brown. She'd sung his song in school a score of times.

"I say," Charlie continued. "I was there. I stood guard on the road that night."

19

"Tell us another, Charlie," Alex taunted in a good-natured way, but Becca kept silent, feeling gooseflesh on her arms, for all the warmth of the day, and gripping her knees in the thrill of revelation, for she sensed the ring of truth in Charlie's voice.

Charlie's story began long after the so-called war in Kansas, when the town of Lawrence had been burned and men had died to bring the territory in as a state. Whether Kansas would be slave or free was the issue. A fugitive with blood on his hands, John Brown had raided Missouri and brought slaves out at gunpoint. While hastening on to Canada and freedom, he had stopped one winter night at the Quaker farm, and Charlie, they now heard, had simply been passing by, but agreed to stand watch on the icy, moonlit road. Who would suspect a boy of fifteen?

"Why didn't you tell us before this?" Becca asked, and Charlie just shrugged.

"Why did you do it at all?" Alex asked. "That Brown was dangerous."

"I suppose because I can't stand anyone not being free," Charlie said. "I wouldn't wish slavery on any man, white or black."

"What happened to the Quakers?" Becca asked.

"I heard they had some threats, and I suppose that's why they left," Charlie said.

Becca had not completely made up her mind about slavery. It was a peculiar institution, all right, and she did not much like the way Southerners could send their agents north after fugitive slaves.

"I don't hate Southerners," Charlie added, "but I hate what they're doing to this country."

"I expect they hate what this country's trying to do to them,"

Alex replied. "I mean, it is the law. They have the right." He was referring to the legal pursuit of runaways. Except for that, he had not thought much about slavery, either. There were few negroes in southern Michigan, and it wasn't an issue in his own life.

"If I were old enough to vote," Charlie said, "I'd vote for Honest Abe in a shot."

"I don't know," Alex mused. "You'd think there might be a middle ground between North and South."

Becca kept silent. The upcoming election meant little to her, though she knew the entire country was embroiled in it. "Let's not spoil the picnic with politics," she said at last. "It's only once a year, and here we are, the three of us. That's mighty special."

"All of us young and healthy," Alex agreed.

"And happy. A great team," Charlie concurred, and threw his arms around the other two. Becca sat very still, feeling the weight of his arm on her shoulders as the wagon clattered past dried rows of cornstalks, the last traces of man's puny gnawings before Thompson's Wood and its soaring gloom. Bare oaks were interspersed with fading maples and towering black walnuts as the first ramparts of the woods engulfed them.

"There," Charlie pointed out the sunlight flashing off the river, and Becca's shoulders, where his arm had been, felt suddenly chilly.

"Oh," she forced herself to say, "it is hot for October. I'm mighty thirsty. I hope you packed plenty of lemonade."

"All shaken up. We'll pour it down, eat the apples, and explode together," Charlie laughed.

Several wagons and buggies already clustered under the enormous trees. Becca climbed down and spread her arms, taking in the deep shade like a swimmer. Dazzled, she tripped over a root and fell, landing in the soft wreckage of countless summers. She was breathless when Alex helped her to her feet.

With a blanket spread, they pooled their treasures. The cold chicken was Ma's doing, along with apples that Becca and her younger brothers had picked only days before. Alex produced gingersnaps wrapped in a napkin, while Charlie unveiled a cool jug of lemonade and three tin cups. "Bet you thought I'd forget the cups," he said.

Nearby came the rustle and dribble of a spring feeding into the river. Beyond the fringe of trees, the sun dappled on the water. None of them could have guessed how often this moment would be dredged up from memory—those autumn tastes and smells, the lingering warmth of Indian summer. It was a last glimpse of Eden, though they did not know it then.

In Jonesville, the band was tuning up its instruments. Politicians thumbed their notes. Wide-Awakes fashioned torches and unrolled their banners for the coming night, and the morning's unsullied clouds piled up into aching thunderheads.

# THREE

## Night of the Abolitionists

THE AIR WAS SULTRY THAT NIGHT. There was a dusty smell to it, as if a spark dropped anywhere might set the world ablaze. As Becca and her two escorts rode back from Thompson's Wood, the sun rolled low over the horizon, where the clouds formed up into medieval domes and vast banners blazing across the sky. The sun did not set that evening, but burst on a pillar of cloud. Once the birds had retreated into the treetops and the light had thickened, full of hidden colors, bats appeared, stitching recklessly through the darker spaces.

The ball had already begun when Becca arrived on the arms of Alex and Charlie. Becca was an excellent dancer and loved going to dances. For a town of some two thousand people, Jonesville had its share of balls. The Waverly House always held a spring cotillion, a Fourth of July ball, and this harvest dance, which she had missed last year when right in the middle of rhetoric class her seatmate had to be sent home, only to die on Friday, the day of the ball. Remembering the shock and suddenness of death's assault, Becca shivered, seeing for an instant behind her eyes the pale face and burning eyes of the Gypsy child.

She forced herself to think of the last dance she'd attended, given by the Freemasons in the Templars' Hall. She'd never missed a set, till three in the morning, when rain made the roads so bad that she and her brother Frank had to stay over with friends. They had sung and played the melodeon until breakfast before starting for home.

Now Becca moved down the chain of hands, lightly, discreetly, her eyes slightly averted, a faint glow on her cheeks. Her first partner was Alex, who moved like a clockwork man: the right steps, but each one of them by solemn rote. Charlie, on the other hand, sensed the tempo with grinning acrobatic invention. She never knew what to expect with Charlie and wished only that she might combine the two into a perfect partner.

Becca could happily have danced the night away, but Jonesville was simply too excited. From the tavern, voices rose louder and louder, and the abolitionist band, which had been playing all afternoon at the depot, formed up and began whang-banging down Main Street, drowning the fiddles until the dance floor emptied.

Jonesville's speaker that night, Cassius Clay of Lexington, Kentucky, was a Yale graduate and cousin to the famous Henry Clay. He'd founded a newspaper back home, *The True American*, dedicated to the abolition of slavery in a slave state, and defended his offices with two four-pound cannon and a keg of black powder. When Clay suddenly fell ill, his opponents took advantage of his absence, invaded the newspaper office, dismantled his printing equipment, and shipped it to Cincinnati before Clay could rise from his sickbed.

The town hall was already packed when Becca, Alex, and Charlie slipped inside. She recognized a good many faces, but there were many strangers in the crowd, and rumor had it that ruffians from Missouri meant to drive Clay from the stage, no easy trick, as he was six feet three, with long arms, big wrists, and a shock of black hair that threatened to impair his vision. In a sudden hush, he strode up to the lectern to stand under a banner emblazoned LINCOLN, LIBERTY, AND UNION, NOW AND FOREVER, ONE AND INSEPARABLE.

"Gentlemen and ladies," he began in a rumbling, crowd-quelling voice. "If there are those among you with respect for God's word, and I trust there are many, I have brought this," and he drew a black Bible from a case at his feet. "And for those who only respect the rules of men, I have brought this." He set a copy of the Constitution beside the Bible. "But if, as I have been advised, there are some among you who respect neither the laws of God nor of men, be apprised that I have brought . . ." and Clay pulled from his satchel a pair of long, black pistols and laid them beside the two documents. For good measure, he placed a heavy bowie knife with the pistols. The crowd murmured its astonishment. "Let those who respect none of the above confront me, here and now . . ." He paused, time enough for Charlie to whisper, "I told you we shouldn't miss this," just as Clay concluded, ". . . or let them depart in peace, and may they not stand upon the order of their going."

After such a beginning, the meeting that followed was disappointingly peaceful. Becca would recall few of the details, save one brief exchange with the audience. Clay had pointed out something Lincoln had told him in Peoria, Illinois, regarding human bondage. "What Lincoln said to me was, 'Clay, I've always felt that the man who hoes the corn should eat the corn.' Well, I'd call that simple common sense. What about you folks?"

This invitation to the crowd brought forth a rather slurred, "Clay, would you up and help a runaway nigger?" Clay, with mock seriousness, put his hand to his chin for a moment before replying. "Well, sir, I suppose it would depend on which way he was running." Predictably, this brought laughter. Then a free negro who worked at the depot proclaimed solemnly, "Mr. Clay, I reckon you have a white skin, but, sir, you have a black heart." Even Clay broke down with laughter at this point, and only reestablished his composure toward the end, when he spoke of the sacred union of the states. "The Union, our Union," he repeated, shaking his head slowly, like a bulldog that has set its teeth and means to hold on, viselike, until death, "on that ground we must stand fast, in which case the glory will be ours to share."

Rebecca Case never pretended to be a historian. But standing there in the press of that resounding hall two weeks before the presidential election, she felt herself a witness to great events. With torches beginning to flare and the younger men drawing up into ranks, Becca sensed that there was a readiness for violence in the air. Just as a lack of rain set the stage for a forest fire in the Michigan wilderness, so here there was a permission on the wind, a readiness to fight on principle, something which comes seldom, if at all, in the life span of a generation.

Now the abolition band struck up again, and the young men marched into the street, bringing their feet down hard. These were the Wide-Awakes, Lincoln's boys, wearing officer-style caps and carrying fence rails topped with torches or lamps. They had first tramped through Hartford, Connecticut, last spring. Now they paraded like warriors through every Northern town, worrying some, exciting others. Becca was both distressed and alarmed seeing how her friends were drawn to the fierce parade.

Charlie Gregory was purely excited. "I hate to run off, Bec. I hope your ma won't have conniptions if you're out a mite late," and before joining the marchers he gave a quick, disarming kiss right on Becca's lips, then was gone into the crowd before she could respond, save with a glow deepening on her cheeks.

He'll never be a soldier, she thought, he'll never learn how to march, for Charlie rose on his toes, a jaunty step, swinging his arms and rolling his shoulders from side to side. He waved once, then was swallowed up by the autumn night. That would always be Charlie, running off, the echo of laughter. For a second Becca wanted to cry, then she felt Alex's arm around her shoulder. "The crowd's getting rowdy," he said. "Maybe I ought to be driving you home."

"Oh, Alex," she replied.

"It's your ma," he said in his clear, cool voice.

"I know," she sighed. "Time for good girls to be safe in bed. Alex, if you take me home now, you'll miss the fireworks."

"I promised her, Becca. I can see them from the wagon." He bestowed that look that was his smile.

Once out of Jonesville, darkness surrounded them. The sky seemed low and filled with tattered clouds, through which the moon sailed unsteadily. "Look at that moon, Alex. Just look at the full moon tonight!" And Alex looked at the sky.

"There it is again," he said. "Didn't I hear thunder earlier? Maybe it was only the crowd roaring."

"If there's a war, Alex," Becca said suddenly, "will you join up?"

"A war?" he replied, puzzled. "Whatever for?" Her intuition had leaped too far ahead. "Well, I suppose it might be my duty to preserve the Union. I hadn't really considered it, Becca. Me, a soldier?" Alex forced a laugh. The last thing Alex fancied was violence, his own least of all.

"What about Charlie?"

"He likes excitement," Alex mused. "He's always talking about seeing the elephant, but then, he hates to be told what to do."

They had reached the Case farm. A solitary lantern burned in a window.

"I'm sorry you're missing the excitement, Alex."

"It was my pleasure, Becca. You know that."

"I hope because you like me."

Growing up with a person, it was easy to take them for granted, but Alex said, looking away, "I was jealous when Charlie kissed you." He studied the sky, dark clouds in the west that seemed to reach for the moon. "You're very beautiful, Becca."

Her voice turned harsh with surprise. "Alexander Forman, what are you talking about?"

Now he stared boldly at her. "You heard me. You're the prettiest girl in Jonesville." At this she laughed, a forthright laugh of pure surprise and pleasure. "To me you are, and I'd admire to kiss you good night."

It was a dignified salute, which Becca returned with equal solemnity, eyes closed. "There," she said, stepping back. Both accepted a kiss as something sacred, not to be bestowed too easily.

"Good night, Becca," Alex said, taking her hands. "Fetching you home was the best part of the evening. Now I ought to be getting Father's horse back."

Becca did not delay him, but she lingered by the road, listening to the clip-clop of the retreating horse, slow at first, then faster. She smiled, thinking, He still wants to catch the excitement. She'd had enough for one night: a first kiss, and not one, but two. Becca had often imagined the shock of being kissed by a boy, yet both had seemed so gentle and natural, though one was too quick, the other too apologetic, as if afraid of waking something in her. Still, they would remain forever the first, and on such a night of excitement in Jonesville. There would be nothing quite like this again, and for a long moment she leaned on the gate, lost in the miracle of it all. Later, with time to reflect, she would confide to her diary, "After all, a kiss should not be taken lightly, even if Mr. Gregory treats it otherwise."

Only the distant mutter of thunder aroused her, and listening for more thunder, Becca heard the singing, faint at first, then growing. A dog barked from a neighbor's porch as the song rose, almost supernatural somehow, like the voice of Jehovah echoing down from the last stars. It was the new tune become so popular this summer, which she had sung at school, "John Brown's Body." So the Wide-Awakes were out marching still.

Becca shivered. She had never felt so alive, so little ready for sleep. All this excitement, and two boys courting her now. She crossed the porch and entered the twilight of the front hall, went on into the deeper dusk of the parlor. She could scarcely make out the forms of things. At least Ma was not sitting up in the dark. Sarah Case had a habit of sniffing slightly but constantly when awake, but the house was still. Becca was being trusted for a change, or probably it was Alex who had her mother's confidence. In any event, there was none of Ma's, "That's enough of you today, Rebecca," or, "Well, I never, Becca Case, never in all my born days," and the greatest humiliation of all, having her wrist tightly grasped in Ma's small, dry hand and being marched in silent fury faster and faster to her bedroom, with all the dignity of a dog on the end of a leash.

Pa was out, as usual, watching the Wide-Awakes or, more likely, at the tavern with a schooner of beer in hand, declaiming on politics or reminiscing over horse races past or speculating upon races yet to be run. Becca glanced around at all the shadowy, familiar objects, which, for ever so long, had been her task to dust once a week, and the big, hooked rug, which had to be hauled out and beaten spring and fall. It was that time again, as soon as things settled down.

Lamp in hand, Becca climbed to the second floor, turned left into her own room, and confronted her face in the wood-framed mirror that sat on the dresser. Her hair did look fine in the golden light—but those horrid big ears! Her father had joked about there being an elf up the family tree. Becca flounced her hair forward and stuck her tongue out at the mirror image. Then she turned to her journal and the page dated October 24, 1860.

With her pen thrust down into a small brass inkwell, Becca rested her chin in one hand and fixed her eyes on the lined blank page of the book, waiting for her thoughts to come. "Pleasant day," she wrote. It was Becca's nature to understate. "To the annual picnic with Alex and Charlie, then to the Waverly House ball. I only danced two sets before Mr. Clay's speech which was uplifting. There were a good many companies of Wide-Awakes and this was a grand show for Jonesville. Alex brought me home at ten and so we missed the fireworks."

So much for October 24, 1860, and yet it seemed to deserve more. Again Becca dipped her pen, adding, "I have only been fifteen for a little over six months and I am far too young for love, still everything must be recorded in this dear journal. I often think no living soul will ever see what it contains but then again I expect to die some time and unless I request all my journals to be burned to ashes, I assume every line will meet the eyes of someone." Following this she wrote only, "Alex???? Charlie????" Of course she was too young to be serious, but what girl needed more than Alex and Charlie? The day would come when she would have to choose.

Alex was handsome and steady, like his hard-working father. Had his mother, Catherine Simmons McCarthy, left no imprint upon him? Kate Forman, as she was called, had brought a son, William McCarthy, into her second marriage. Much older than Alex, Bill had gone off to work as a blacksmith for the railroad, taking the mystery of his creation with him. If Mrs. Forman could have clarified her past, in her English accent, for the enrichment of the Jonesville mythology, she chose not to do so.

Yes, Becca was very fond of Alex. She was not at all sure how she could do without him, but part of her was ready to run off with Charlie, who would look at a map, find a blank space, then put down his finger saying, "One day." How could she ever give up Charlie Gregory, yet how dare she commit all of herself to him?

Alex and Charlie, Charlie and Alex. The names played in her head until, abruptly, Becca sat forward and stared into the black square of the window. She seemed to see cards laid out like the branching arms of a cross. Was her choice the wandering fool on one hand, a sad journey into maternity on the other, while over all loomed the implacable figure of death? She would make no such choice. Why not stay an old maid, remain her own woman to the end, accept none of those binding obligations, be no man's wife and no one's mother. Becca sat back and took a deep, comforting breath. She could still fool fate and the Gypsies by staying Rebecca Case forever, safe and on her own.

Becca remained at the table long after she had closed her journal. Outside the last stars were gobbled up and the storm arrived with a roar, scattering the Wide-Awakes, extinguishing their torches, encouraging the revelers to go another round while belting out a last chorus of "John Brown's Body," loud and off-key, by which time Becca had turned down her lamp and retired. Through the rain that fell abruptly and hard, she seemed to hear the song coming with trancelike dignity, filtering through the blustering night to reach her, its melody rising and falling like wind at the keyhole.

Burst firecrackers moldered in the puddles. Guttered black stumps of discarded torches littered the roadside. The old Mexican War cannon in the square still bore a blackened mouth from all the salutes. A train pulled out of the depot, heading east, with Cassius Clay aboard, tired, but confident that he was leaving behind another small town safely in Lincoln's camp. One by one Jonesville dimmed its lights and began to snore. By this time Becca was asleep.

# FOUR

# To See the Elephant

AFTER CASSIUS CLAY AND THE Wide-Awakes, Lincoln's election came as an anticlimax, not to be compared with Becca's trip to Dr. Hobby, who used chloroform to ease the extraction of an aching tooth. She was too busy before Christmas, making toys and pulling molasses candy, to dwell on South Carolina's withdrawal from the Union or consider the implications of Charleston's federal garrison's retreat to Fort Sumter in the harbor.

January saw Becca going back to school, being initiated into the Order of the Eastern Star, and making a dress to wear to her older brother Douglas's wedding. "I sewed like a goodfellow today," she informed her journal. Becca would miss Douglas, and she wondered if his quiet, frail Julia was a wise choice. She told her journal only that "Douglas and his beloved Julia will take up boarding out at Pulaski in February."

Meanwhile, January saw other states abandon the Union. Such politics had nothing to do with Becca or her journal, nor did Jefferson Davis's taking office as president of the Confederacy of Southern states. Lincoln was inaugurated in early March. Becca was not sure of the date. She inserted in her diary, "I wonder if anything serious will befall him. I hope not." There was so much angry talk about so many Southern states leaving the Union that the Michigan legislature was considering calling up the militia.

Then came Friday, April 12, so sunny with springtime that Becca wore her sunbonnet to the dentist, who filled eight cavities with gold leaf. "In the old days, we'd have used lead," Dr. Hobby told her. Becca felt a bit shaky on leaving, but managed tea with Alex later, and wrote that evening, "My teeth feel fine."

While Becca recorded her small, somewhat trying day, Jonesville was ceasing to drift in the brown plowed fields of southern Michigan, for the outside world was about to reach over and touch the place and all who lived there. It did so in the form of a special issue of the *Jonesville Weekly Independent*, which shouted in headlines two inches tall, black staccato slashes of ink. The Confederates had fired and kept on firing at Fort Sumter, until the garrison surrendered for want of food. No casualties were reported until a cannon exploded while discharging a final salute. All Charleston turned out, ecstatically waving flags, shooting off squibs, and wearing palmetto cockades in their hats.

Becca's father read the news aloud, then banged down the paper. "This is an affront to the flag of the United States!" he said.

Jonesville was wild with excitement. Little boys beat on tin-pan drums, and that Sunday the church organ tuned up with patriotic melodies. "They call it Star Spangled Fever," Becca wrote in her journal.

As Pa explained it: "This country hasn't got an army fit to make up a backwoods 'Posse comitatus,' let alone fight any kind of war." And while Becca was telling her diary on April 15, "Rather pleasant, no news," President Lincoln was calling for seventy-five thousand volunteers. They were to serve for ninety days, time enough to set the Union back in order. Just about every young man in Jonesville said he wanted to enroll, and according to the paper, it was like that throughout the North, with no time to lose. Rumor held that Baltimore was in rebel hands and that only Cassius Clay's arrival in Washington with a few hundred volunteers had saved the capital. Michigan sent out a call for ten companies of volunteers, and at Sunday-evening service Becca heard the minister urging Jonesville's sons to do their duty. Though most of them were far too young, Becca couldn't name a boy in school who wasn't ready to fight. But against whom? Did that even matter? They just wanted to go off and do glorious deeds, to "see the elephant," as the older ones put it.

According to Charlie, a fat old doctor was asking the older boys if they ever had spasms or piles, and if they answered no, he judged them fit to sign up for thirteen dollars a month, good pay for the unemployed. When the time came, they'd be shipped off to Grand Rapids, where the first three Michigan regiments were already training and, according to the paper, taking to army life "as natural as a three-months' calf to a pail of warm milk."

For those awaiting the official call, there was fierce-faced marching on the common, conducted by a self-appointed German drill sergeant: "Eyes front, toes out, leedle finger mid de seam de bantaloons. Ach, dummkopfs, you nebber make soldiers!" Becca loved it all, confiding in her diary, "It seems as though we never were alive until now." On May 23, while Virginia was finally voting itself out of the Union, Becca found herself at the Templars' Hall, trying on the red-white-and-blue apron of the Florence Nightingale Association, which meant that she would be knitting head-and-neck covers called havelocks.

Next day, Becca stood at the depot where the Coldwater company of volunteers sang, "It is sweet, it is sweet, for one's country to die," while the mayor solemnly told them that "the eagle of American liberty, from her mountain eyrie, has warned us of danger. Now she swoops down on spreading pinions. She has perched on this banner which we now give to your keeping." In response, the colonel said the flag would never be surrendered, while the boys pledged not to return until the banner waved triumphantly over Dixie. Flags were all over town, and that night Becca and her friends sewed a banner for the schoolhouse cupola.

Thereafter the excitement died down. No one seemed to know when the Jonesville volunteer company would be activated, yet when Alex came by, looking even more serious than usual, she assumed he had something to tell her about the Seventh Michigan. "Not really," he said. Alex had never been among the more exuberant volunteers. To him it was duty. "I did see Jim Schriber, though," he told her. "His pa gave him a new sword and told him not to bring it back until it was stained to the hilt."

"With blood?" Becca said. "Poor Jim."

"Becca, we have to talk," Alex said. He didn't much like bets or dares, or keeping secrets, but Charlie had put him up to it, and he was painfully embarrassed. Why had he gotten into this? Becca was pretty, but she wasn't beautiful, nor was she that amusing or compassionate. She could cook, but so could all the girls. You didn't fall in love with a girl for her cooking, and so Alex had accepted that there was no answer except that he was in love with Becca Case and had been for ever so long.

Becca's eyes were down. Her face looked closed when he said, "Becca, I love you." Alex thought at first she had not heard him. Perhaps it was just as well.

In fact Becca seemed to guess what Alex was going to say in advance, yet somehow she was surprised. Finally she raised her eyes and lightly touched his arm. "Oh, Alex," she replied, and that was all.

"It's just that if I get my father's consent and join up, well, the company might move out at any time, and I wondered whether you'd consider waiting for me."

"Is that a proposal?" she asked him, a spot of red having appeared on both her cheeks, to which he nodded, not trusting himself to speak. "Alex, you're a nice boy."

"It's not fair to say that."

"Alex, it's only that we're far too young. I am. My folks would never hear of it." In fact, she was not absolutely sure of this. Pa might have just shrugged, and Ma, though she was protective, thought well of Alex.

"I suppose you're right," Alex agreed. Was there relief in his voice, she wondered? Then he said, almost as an afterthought, "When I come home, if I do, I mean to try again. I'll be upset if you say yes to anyone else meanwhile."

"Anyone else?" she echoed, puzzled.

"Well, Charlie Gregory, for one."

"He's not the marrying kind," she replied.

"You may be surprised," Alex countered.

Becca was not thinking of this conversation when Charlie came the next day. "Well, we've got a name," he told her. "Company C, the Jonesville Light Guard. And we've got officers." Company C had chosen Henry Baxter as captain. "I think the chances are we'll be going soon."

"Going?"

"To Fort Wayne, for real training. It's at Detroit." Charlie gazed confidently up at the blue sky so empty and free for his future deeds. "Bec, have you time for a walk?"

It was hot, and presently they found themselves barefoot

in the shallows of the Saint Joseph River, dragging their feet in the water, stirring up little waves, so interested in the game that they did not look where they were going and bumped together. Then Charlie turned and faced her, seized both her hands in his, and took aim with a kiss.

"Charlie!" she protested, stepping back. Only his grasp kept her from falling.

"I've got you," he said, smiling. "And now, Miss Mousie, as the song goes, will you marry me?"

"Don't make fun, Charlie."

"I'm not," he insisted. "Say yes, and I'll stay home from the war, settle down, become postmaster one day, all the trimmings."

"Don't be silly," Becca protested, more by reflex than anything else. "I'm barely sixteen. Pa'd skin you. Imagine what Ma would say."

Charlie grimaced. "I'd hate to hear it, but you sure are pretty when you blush like that."

"Everyone's been telling me that lately," Becca replied.

"Well, it's true," and Charlie seemed so pleased that he extended a finger and traced the line of her eyebrow, roughing it gently against the grain until Becca shivered. For some reason she was reminded of the time with the Gypsies. "And if you're not for marriage," he added, undismayed, "what say you to running off to California?"

"You and me?"

"Who else? And look for gold."

"Is that a proper thing to ask a decent girl?"

"Faint heart ne'er won fair lady." Charlie laughed. "I hadn't thought about it that way. I'm mad about you, Bec. I am."

"Hush, Charlie," she replied, but was smiling now.

"Sure beats getting shot all to hell, begging your pardon, and I'm just the one to stop a bullet, I am." Then, when this appeal for sympathy did not seem to be gaining ground, he added seductively, "Let's go, Bec. Come on with me. It's now or never."

"We'd starve out there."

"But we wouldn't be bored. I could raise sheep or cattle or something, and you'd grow corn. Nights, we'd listen to the Indians drumming in the hills."

Becca's head was in a whirl. She saw herself stepping off a precipice yet was very nearly ready to close her eyes to the consequences, and that part of her that her conscience regarded as the dark side seemed to whisper, "Quick, quick, speak, or he will be gone." She did not speak, nor did he depart, but the moment was soon past.

"Well, you know me, Bec," Charlie said. "Like as not, I'll turn to drink out of pure despair. But I'll try to wait, so long as you don't say yes to Alex."

"What?" Becca asked. She hadn't really heard Charlie.

"Believe me, if you and Alex were plunked down in the Garden of Eden, instead of Adam and Eve, you'd still be there."

"May I ask, is that so bad?" Becca was putting two and two together. She smelled a conspiracy. All this proposing had been rehearsed in advance. "You and Alex planned this, isn't that so?"

Charlie seemed to collect himself for a great lie or a great confession, then said, "There's such trust in your eyes, Bec." Finally he admitted the bet between himself and Alex, adding, "I guess we both lose," to which Becca laughed, puzzled. Her lips remained parted, waiting to understand the joke. "You see, we're both sincere about you, Bec." When he saw her biting her lip with vexation, he added, "I guess we didn't get off on the right foot."

"No, I believe it's in your mouth," she told him. Becca felt humiliated, not wanting anything to do with either of them just now, not knowing whether to laugh or cry, and finally coming out with a laugh that was close to a sob. "And you're the worst, making me feel like an idiot. Go away."

"Admit it, Bec, you're a little sweet on me. Please, Bec."

"Go away and get yourself killed in the silly army. See if I care," and before she could stop him, he went.

That was the first week of June. A recruiting wagon rolled through Jonesville that same day with a fifer and drummer aboard, followed by new recruits shouting, "Fourth of July every day of the year!" By now Becca had long regretted her sharpness. Bet or no, the proposals had been sincere enough. When the boys came around with a poem, half serious, half sad, which ended, "Oh, we hope, yes we hope you'll forgive us sometime," she had replied, "Would I be foolish to forgive you right now?" She said this sternly but with a smile already in her mind, if not yet on her lips. Then Becca did forgive them both, recording their poem in her journal that night.

Events moved swiftly now. On June 8 Alex showed her his father's consent, and with the rank of corporal, he was ushered into Company C, Seventh Michigan Volunteers, Captain Henry Baxter commanding. There was a rush to the daguerre-otype artist, as Becca called the Jonesville photographer. "You do look stern," she told Alex. For his likeness Alex had thrust one hand inside his uniform blouse in approved Napoléon fashion, but then, he bore the dignity of rank.

"You ought to see Charlie. Revolver in one hand, bowie knife in the other. Fierce as a pirate."

"Charlie. I bet he could barely keep from laughing," she replied.

Alex visited Becca on June 18. He was due to leave the following day with the chosen officers for preliminary training at Fort Wayne. On this solemn occasion, he presented her with his likeness and a lock of hair. She in turn pressed upon him a blue necktie and a carryall, called a housewife, made of morocco leather. She waved back at his white handkerchief for over half a mile as his train pulled away from Jonesville.

On July 1 eight weeks of summer vacation began for Becca with the usual school picnic. Three weeks later, in Virginia, came the war's first great battle, Bull Run, or Manassas, as the Confederates called it after their resounding victory. "The Great Skedaddle" was its name in the Union army. This news, together with the president's call for one hundred thousand more volunteers, Becca recorded in her diary, concluding her entry, "No more shouting of 'On to Richmond.' I hope the Seventh never is called." She soothed herself with this hope for about a fortnight.

Then Alex returned, officially the Seventh Michigan's bugler now. "We're not home for long," he confided, and on August 13 Becca found herself beside her father in the buggy, riding off to watch the last parade. "I shall never tire of seeing the soldiers march and drill which they did all morning," she wrote.

That afternoon the regiment, standing in a hollow square, received its colors, sewn by the schoolgirls. The boys sang, "We will rally round the flag" with lusty enthusiasm, while the girls, including Becca, replied, shy at first but coming on strong, "I am bound to be a soldier's wife or die an old maid." "A thoughtful song," she wrote in her diary that night, "and I have taken it very much to heart."

Presently it was time to say good-bye for the last time. All promised to write. "Care of Captain Baxter," Alex reminded her, while Charlie asked, "You wouldn't do anything violent if I kissed you good-bye?" Becca intended only to brush his cheek with her lips, but he took hold of her and drew her into a real kiss. "Well," she said, "I do fear for those Virginia

41

girls." Then, of course, she had to kiss Alex too, and Charlie's example did not disturb the dignity of this last salute, for which Becca knew not whether to be happy or sad.

Captain Henry Baxter marched out front toward the depot and its waiting cars. Swinging around with his gleaming new sword in hand, he glared at the uncertain ranks. "Close up, boys," he ordered. "This is not the harvest picnic, just because you have sweethearts in the crowd."

Becca watched this last innocent parade with her sister-in-law Julia. Douglas was talking about joining up and might have done so already, had not Julia pleaded with him not to.

"I wonder how many will come back," Julia said. To Becca, the Jonesville boys looked so healthy, almost immortal, in their clumsy new blue uniforms, with the big doughnut-shaped blanket rolls and the stiff haversacks already greased with lard, that it seemed impossible that death could ever poison such happy smiles, such sparkling eyes.

"Don't be silly, they all will," Becca insisted, to which Julia simply shook her head. Becca might have remonstrated with her, but then, such was Julia's gloomy nature. Besides, her words would have been wasted, for the boys were singing thunderously, "We are coming, Father Abraham."

The girls who had remembered to do so wore white dresses and were beginning to shiver because this was a solemn occasion—they had yet another flag to present—and because it was beginning to drizzle. At the depot, the red-and-black engine sent its white-hot breath into the trees, fanning the branches upward. The engine was draped with bunting and hung with a silver shield lettered DEATH TO TRAITORS.

As the new soldiers scrambled aboard the cars, Captain Baxter, in a voice that originated in his chest and flowed with a pulpit conviction, admonished them, "Boys, when you and

I have long been forgotten, I want these people to remember and tell their grandchildren, 'You should have heard them singing, you should have seen our boys as they marched away.' " But the cars were just boxcars, with backless benches of rough planks, and the volunteers by now were more interested in passing around bad whiskey, a dollar a pint. For many it was their first serious drink, one they would regret.

"Be careful!" Becca shouted as the train blew its whistle.

"I'll be careful," Alex called back, and Charlie, bottle in hand and grinning broadly, shouted, "No fear for me. Just tell the elephant to look out!"

Becca waved her bonnet as the train jerked into motion. Again their destination was star-shaped Fort Wayne, built in 1843 and a training depot since the first call for volunteers. As soon as the officers demonstrated their ability to command, the troops would join the Army of the Potomac, ready for battle.

That night, rain fell steadily. Frogs and sawing insects celebrated the wet, and Becca thought it was time for a serious session with her journal. Should she have sent her photograph off to war? She kept uniformed likenesses of both Alex and Charlie in the top drawer of her dresser. In fact she'd had a picture taken, but found the result terribly plain and serious. Southern women were said to be bright and fiery, though fickle no doubt. Northern women were unfailingly true and tender, which Becca meant to be, even if having two beaux was a bit of a problem. But it wasn't in the interests of morale to make a choice now.

"Alex is a manly well-behaved young gentleman," she wrote, "and no one can speak the truth and say otherwise. He does not keep his mouth constantly filled with that obnoxious weed or smoke dirty pipes and segars as many of our young gents here do. And worse than all is the poisonous cup. From that also is he exempt."

She would most certainly always love Alex, but was it as a woman should love a husband, or more as a brother? For Alex she felt everything but the excitement of romance. "You're so intense, so serious," she had told him, and Alex, pondering for a moment, had replied, "I'm afraid I always will be."

About Charlie she dared not write. He scarcely figured in Becca's journal. With Charlie it had been love at first sight despite all his flaunted bad habits, like drinking as the train pulled out. Admitting this, Becca admonished herself. With Alex it would just take time, but wasn't it true that the mortar that sets more slowly lasts longer? If she would always love Alex, she might come to hate Charlie by and by. He might come to hate her. They would certainly fight. Yet, for all these reservations, though Becca might call her love for Alex sacred and her feelings for Charlie profane, deep down in that core of illogic which resists all prudence, she sensed as surely as a swan recognizes its mate that Charlie was her true love. None of this went into her journal. Becca, a very rational girl, simply denied it to herself that night, even revived that safe course, "single blessedness," as Ma called it. But with the memory of the Gypsies fading, this possibility seemed to fade, too.

Slowly she pulled off her frock, unbuttoned her boots, stepped out of her petticoats, unhooked her corset, and pulled on a white cotton nightgown before removing her drawers and rolling down her stockings. Annoyed, she saw that the stockings needed darning again. And the hair—as she pulled out all the hairpins and began to brush, it hardly seemed worth the trouble of putting it up.

One day, Becca felt she would have to choose. If the war served no other function, it at least deferred that decision. The day was over, and Becca felt she would never go back to where she had been before. They were the same old clothes, but she was different, and once she put them on again, all would be forever altered. She had no doubt of it. She put down the brush and, as usual, knelt by her bed to say her prayers.

# FIVE

---

# *Soldiers and Deserters*

It SEEMED TO Becca that an odd calm settled over Jonesville once her two soldier boys had gone away, even a kind of lazy comfort. After all, they were not yet in peril, and she enjoyed writing and receiving letters. One could think twice about what one said in letters.

This was the time of year when, if Becca listened, she could hear the fall, one by one, of apples, until they seemed to drop like rain, painting the ground crimson. She loved the colors and the clear autumn weather. The singing of skylarks seemed to lift the clear blue, blinding sky higher and higher toward the sun.

On October 22 she wrote in her journal, "Father bought a Gypsy pony this week and I enjoyed as pleasant a ride on its back this afternoon as I ever remember of having and for the fact that t'was such an easy riding one, I rode five miles into the country." She had trotted out past the Jonesville cemetery, where the old, rotting wooden crosses were being replaced with marble slabs. Of her people only great-uncle Jedediah Bolen was buried there, the family pioneer who

46

came out on horseback, with a long-barreled rifle across his saddle. Now the Indian grass, gone red with frost, rippled and moaned above him and the early dead of Jonesville's first generation.

"I don't want to lie there, ever," Becca told herself, and turned the pony for home. With no festival this autumn, because of the war, the Gypsies had drifted away, and she met no one on the road. Yet when a partridge flew up from cover, her mount started, and a chill went through her. Becca controlled her panic as she controlled the pony. Even if it had been those people, even if she had heard them call *kiahli*, she would have ridden on slowly, with dignity.

Becca's father, helping her rub down the pony after her return, said with a laugh, "I hear Charlie Gregory's back in town. Seems his going to serve old Uncle Sam was just some kind of prank."

"Prank?" Becca echoed.

"Well, I don't blame him. There's not a whole lot of future in soldiering."

It suddenly seemed to Becca that Charlie was a stranger whose actions she could not predict. I don't really know him, she realized with a flash of panic, nor did she, in her confusion, want to see him. When he came out to visit that afternoon, standing politely by the front gate, her first thought was to hide in her room and plead a sick headache. Instead she went to meet him with upright head and squared shoulders.

Charlie looked like one who was outdoors all of every day, and he looked glad to be alive. "I'm back," he said with a special edition of the Gregory grin, and, just in time, Becca froze an answering smile that had begun to spread across her face.

"So I see," she told him, "and don't go on about how you

can't stand being away from me and all that. You signed up with the company; you took an oath. Oh, Charlie, you'll get in such trouble. Why?"

He shrugged. "I have all sorts of answers. Take your pick."

"But you've deserted. They shoot soldiers for that."

"Happily, no," he replied. "I wouldn't do that." Charlie was not one to harbor things in his heart. "I went as a kind of lark. Look, Bec, if you want the truth, you'll have it. It may make you mad."

"I don't get mad at the truth," she said in a voice brittle with irritation.

"The truth is, I never did sign up," Charlie explained. "For one thing, I'm not good at taking orders. I'm not meant for soldiering, you know that."

"There's such a thing as obeying orders."

"I obey my own conscience, Bec."

"So you think you're morally superior to other people?"

"No, but this is what'll bother you, Bec. I mean, I guess it's too bad to break up the Union after seventy-odd years, but I don't hate Southerners. Seems to me they have the right to go their own way."

For all the excitement and fine words of the summer past, Becca had given the right and wrong of it little thought. If called, was it not one's unquestioned duty to serve one's country? Didn't that free one from one's own conscience?

"Guess I'm not very good at doing what I'm told," Charlie admitted.

"But your country needs you."

Charlie gave her a half-smile. "Well, it's good to be needed by someone. But then, Bec, what's a country? Some earth surrounded on all sides by boundaries, mostly unnatural ones. I'd fight like a demon if I had a cause. Believe me, I'd be as

48

patriotic as all getout if we were fighting to free the slaves. Remember what Cassius Clay said last fall—if you hoe the corn you ought to be the one to eat the corn?"

"I don't know any negroes," Becca said. "I've never thought much about all that," though she had heard her father praise the African American Colonization Society, which sent freed slaves back to Africa. "And I still think you're wrong, Charlie. I'm sorry, but I can't help it," and she turned and went into the house. Charlie watched her, his mouth open as if to speak. His hands rose and fell back to his sides. Then he, too, turned, and headed back down the road.

On the same day, Becca received a letter from Alex. It was dated September 15, 1861, Meridian Hill, Washington, D.C.

Dear Becca,

I have now seized my first chance of writing since I left home. We arrived in Pittsburg after dark and again came another delay of two or three hours. Our next journey lay through the Alleghany Mountains and such beautiful scenery never before beheld. We soon arrived at Baltimore "that rebel city" where the first blood of Freedom's sons was shed in this unholy struggle. The 7th passed through without any of the welcome received by our predecessors but they were kept back, or rather checked by fifteen or 20,000 U.S. troops stationed there. It was Sunday when we arrived and we marched through Baltimore, our band playing the usual national airs. We met with many frowns, but out of some windows waved the "stars and stripes." We left there in the afternoon and soon arrived in the renowned city of Washington. Here we passed the first night on the warehouse floor. We are in the midst of death at all times. Pies have been taken away from Peddlers and poison found in them, and the murderers were arrested. The water has also been found in the same fix. . . .

His next letter, dated October 1, came from Camp Benton, Maryland. Alex wrote;

It is all hills and vales, and huge forests among which are found the Oak, Chestnut and Persimmon trees, but I really do not know what to think of the soil. It may be productive but it is not to my taste. It is red clay and during rainy weather one can scarcely walk it is so slippery. Last night our batteries amused themselves by throwing a few shells into their breast works. This they do most every day, or else they would soon have it strongly fortified, which would not answer at all for our business, for all things tend to show that we will soon cross over there and drive them out. Don't you think we will have gay times doing it?

Alex seldom had a chance to write until nightfall, using his knapsack as a desk.

Dear Becca,

I begin to think this war means to keep us all waiting forever. Long drills in the cold, target practice with our old Belgian smooth bores. Believe me, a barn door would be safe at 100 yards if it hadn't already gone for fire wood. Right now we are having a warm spell. Some accordian music is very pleasing under a bright moon but despite this spell of good weather we spend much free time building winter quarters. The walls are 8 logs high with shake roofs and sleeping bunks on the side with a big fireplace. I hope you agree we'll have a fine home this winter. Now a fiddle has struck up and there's a pair of bones beginning to tap. Some fellows have commenced singing "Happy Land of Canaan." Yes, there are a few things about this camp life I shall miss while all the time yearning for home or at the very least a test of strength with Johnny Reb. There are rumors that General Johnson is moving his rebels back to Fairfax Courthouse and there is again shouting of "On to Richmond." Now we have General McClellan to lead us. Some of the boys call him The Happy Warrior or Little Napoleon and he is well liked by all. I can tell you he cuts a fine figure prancing about the camps on a big black bay called "Daniel Webster."

Tomorrow, according to rumor, we are off to scout the Potomac near Leesburg, where a small rebel force has been slow to withdraw. No contact is expected as they can be no match for us.

It is growing late, Becca. You might now find the camp a pretty place, full of mysterious song. If Charlie were here he might call it a forest lit by glowworm light, or he might deem it evil, for the dark figures moving against the cooking fires resemble pictures of Hell as seen in the family Bible. There, a German band has struck up "Morgenroth." The melody spreads. The night reverberates with it. Soon I must close as the bugle will be sounding "Extinguish Lights." Believe me, I have no dread of laying down my life for my country if need be. I fear only that if this waiting goes on and on, you will presently forget me. As for myself, I have no chance of doing so, and every thought of home is associated with some thought of you. There, I hear the last bugle and so good night and happy dreams.

Alex, U.S.A.

Becca was prompt to reply to her soldier boy. Much of Alex's news she passed along to Charlie. The Seventh Michigan might not yet be fighting, she told him, but were they not taking chances with typhoid fever, which raged through the Army of the Potomac that autumn?

After a long silence, Charlie observed, "Bec, I'd never make a good soldier. I'm just no good at taking orders. I'd take my chances against wild Indians, stampeding buffalo, blizzards, but I couldn't stand drilling and having somebody tell me who I should hate."

"That's running away, Charlie Gregory."

"No, Bec, it's running to something. We could have anything we want."

"Not that way."

"The whole world, Bec. Don't you trust me?"

"I know you, Charlie. I've grown up with you," to which he gave back a clear-eyed, smiling face that said, Come on, I'm no threat, not old Charlie. Then he did an odd thing. He ran his fingers through her hair gently, the fingers forming a rough comb, and after a while he whispered, "Such hair, Bec; it's like—I'm not sure—a waterfall—no, more like a mountain mist."

"It's a nuisance," she replied, frozen into taut immobility.

"It's the ocean. I believe I could swim in your hair." She might well have melted entirely had Charlie not added, "And look what I've found: a ship lost in the waves."

"What foolishness." She had closed her eyes, opening them to realize he was referring to her right ear. Quickly Becca drew the hair forward.

"Don't," he said. "It's a marvelous ear."

"It's a great big ugly ear," she insisted, "and I hate it."

"Well, I love it, Bec, and when we get to San Francisco I'll dig up some gold nuggets and have them made into ear bobs."

Beyond the apple orchard, evening was turning from red to green, the clouds opening to reveal great cavities of sky. For a moment Becca, gazing with Charlie's eyes, saw mountains, and beyond them the sea, for she wanted them to be mountains and the sea. Swiftly night thickened. The red clouds were edged with gold, then purple, great sailing ships and swans, fabulous oriental dragons of spun silver and torn silk, until the sunset faded and with the darkness came reality.

"I can just see myself in gold earrings, all rouged up like those fancy women on the train." Bound for the West's dens of iniquity, as Ma would say. "Honestly, Charlie, I don't know what to say to you. I'm not accusing you of running away, but. . . ."

And with this he stood accused.

"Are you calling me a coward, Bec?"

"Don't be silly. That's just how it looks to some people."

"I don't care about some people, Bec, I care about you," he said, almost pleading.

"I can't see inside you, Charlie." Charlie stood there, listening. She might have been pelting him with rotten eggs, but he kept a fixed smile and said nothing.

When Becca finally fell silent, Charlie stared at the ground. "Well," he said at last, "I guess I know where I stand." His eyes fixed hers. There was no further appeal in them. "Got to go," he added. After a pause like a heartbeat, Charlie strode to the gate. There he turned, saying, "I'll see you in gold ear bobs yet," and squared his shoulders as if he had made up his mind.

Becca watched him, his name in her mind, if not on her lips. She was angry, more at herself than at Charlie, and presently she scratched furiously in her diary, "All this fuss about negroes. Women work harder than slaves, how about our being emancipated?" This was her one outburst of feminism, ever. She was soon feeling guilty. Just suppose everyone felt like Charlie; there would be no more war. Yet, to think this seemed such disloyalty to Alex that she went on with her journal, "I would really like to see my good old friend Alex to-night. But he is doing more good where he is endeavoring to fight with many other brave lads for our blessed union than if he were in my society. I don't suppose he hardly can think of me so far away. Though I trust that when he is thinking of his many friends at home he will permit me to occupy a small corner near his heart. It matters not what I tell you my truest best friend for you have always proved trustworthy. To you my heart secrets have all been unfolded. Try and be as faithful as ever. I must banish gloom away and bid you dear journal good-night."

The following morning her father returned with the newspaper full of the disaster at Ball's Bluff. On October 21 the Confederates had routed General Stone's Union force above the Potomac River and had driven them back in such confusion that many drowned. The field commander, Colonel Edward Baker, a former senator and a friend of the president, was among the dead. The newspaper concluded with this snippet of a poem:

> Aye, deem us proud, for we are more
> Than proud of all our mighty dead.

Mighty dead? The paper had said they'd run like frightened sheep, which mattered little to Becca, who cared only for Alex and all the other poor boys from Jonesville left floundering in the Potomac below Ball's Bluff. It would take days for such specific news to arrive from Washington, and for the first time, Becca began really to doubt her convictions about the war. She even decided to tell Charlie so, the next time she saw him, but Charlie did not come by that day or the next.

Becca wondered if he were sulking at home. It was said of the Gregorys that they were either way up, or way down in the dumps. Charlie's twin, Ephraim, had a taste for drink and had spent a night in jail on that account. An older schoolmate had told her that Ephraim had threatened to kill himself before he had vanished from Jonesville. Becca pictured Charlie in such a state and so talked herself into visiting the Gregory home in search of reassurance, but when she got there, Charlie was gone. "These two days," his mother said, her eyes swollen with tears. "Two days, and not a word."

# SIX

---

# *On to Richmond?*

CHRISTMAS 1861 WAS A CHEERLESS ONE in Jonesville. Most of the boys were gone, and no one said "On to Richmond" anymore. Alex received no furlough home, though the Army of the Potomac idled in winter quarters throughout the holidays. Charlie, too, seemed gone for good—gone west, Becca supposed. The prairies and mountains would be a hard place to be in winter.

Becca stayed at home on New Year's. There were no parties, no ball at the Waverly House. Even her birthday went by unremembered until she approached her journal and noted the date, January 29, 1862, a Wednesday. "Well, it seems I am seventeen years old this very day," she wrote sadly, "and who can believe it. I cannot realize that I'm getting so old. Brothers married and beaux gone to war makes this a gloomy winter for me."

For recreation there was church on Sunday, perhaps a temperance lecture in the evening, but few friends to greet thereafter. With the colder weather, Becca had to shovel snow into the great pot for water for washing clothes, though in February her household tasks were lightened. "We had a girl come today to do the work," Becca noted. "She appears saucy to me." Many of the hired help were working on the army contract at Gardiner's woolen mill.

Often Becca rode to visit her sister-in-law Julia in Pulaski. This was her secret joy. "If I could make the horse canter I could ride easier," she recorded, "but she is one of Pa's trotters and simply refuses. Still I like her because she goes so fast." When hard winter set in, they went by sleigh "taking plenty of hot bricks and buffaloes to keep us warm." On February 5 she duly reported, "I never wanted to go east so bad and thought so much about it but today I am fairly homesick and, worse than all, when I came from school Mother's first words were that Father had traded this place for the Clarendon House."

The next day Becca received a letter. The envelope bore the imprint of an American flag and the legend Long May It Wave, and the return address was "Company C, 7th Mich. Regt, Washington, D.C.," but where she assumed would be the sender's name, A. A. Forman, was printed C. Gregory, private.

The letter began:

Friend Becca,

I bet you never expected Old Charlie would rally to the colors. You may ask how did that scamp get into the regiment so late? Well it's being a close family friend to Capt. Vrooman, who knows I can keep up with the best of them not to mention I can shoot the eye out of a hummingbird let alone Johnny Reb. You will be pleased to hear I am messing with Alex who is fit as a fiddle and some of the other Jonesville boys. You remember Jim Schriber and his shiny new sword. Never did get to use it, just up and died of camp fever. I gave him an overcoat and blanket as there was a mix up and I had a double allowance

57

but he went right on shivering. He didn't want to go to the hospital. Kept saying "If a fellow goes to the hospital you may as well say good-bye." The rest of us are bully and one of the boys is cooking preserved oysters, $1.00 a can from the sutler. For breakfast this morning we had pan cakes. There is talk of moving south soon when the weather clears. So write me a letter by return. After all Bec you talked me into doing "my duty."

> Your friend Charlie the Rover

So Charlie had seen the light. Well, that was right and proper, but there was a measure of guilt behind Becca's first reply, which was followed by others, to both Charlie and Alex, with sweet steadfastness. The whole of C Company recognized the small, precise handwriting in dark blue ink and chided the recipients whenever the letters arrived. To Charlie she wrote:

This is St. Valentine's Day tho' I have not seen or heard of a Valentine. I guess this practice of sending them is nearly done away with and hope so at least. Otherwise sleighing has been fine. I wish all the boys were home to enjoy it.

To Alex:

We hear frequently of deaths near you. Company H 4th Regiment has lost four with measles and typhoid fever.

To which Alex replied:

Today one of our new recruits, a strong hearty fellow died. He was taken with measles, caught cold and now is in his grave. His name was Jas. Williams. I pray God that I may never die and be buried in such a manner. It's the strapping country boys who seem always to fall ill while the thin little fellows from the big cities seldom seem to sicken.

In February, despite the snow and Becca's reluctance, the Case family moved from their farm into town. The *Jonesville Weekly Independent* duly noted that "F. B. Case, our well known 'fast-horse citizen' has taken over the Clarendon House, a stopping place for stages, convenient to Jonesville Trotting Park, with a fine piano and melodeon for the benefit of guests." Because living in town was more like the remembered commotion of Brooklyn, Becca was quick to prefer it to the quiet countryside, though Alex seemed to disapprove of life in a hotel. In a letter, he wrote:

> Give me the pleasure of a quiet home where is not found the busy bustle of "Public Life."

He confessed in the same letter:

> I sometimes feel discouraged, disgusted with camp life. There is nothing good, nothing pleasant but these thoughts ill become me as a soldier.

He slept with his cartridge box over his shoulder, and still the ever-present rats tried to eat the greased cartridges. He complained of their firearms, though General McClellan said new Harpers Ferry rifles were expected before the spring campaign.

> Even better, we are hoping for the Spencer repeaters which you can load in the morning and shoot all day long. Becca, we have had a stripe added to our regimental banner with the

motto "Tuebor" emblazoned in gold thread. And Becca, would it be an imposition to ask, could you perhaps find me a pair of mittens with the first finger separate to handle a rifle? Like this [Here Alex painstakingly produced a sketch of a mitten with thumb and index finger separate].

No such convenience existed in the shops of Jonesville, so Becca set to work with knitting needles, an occupation for which she had, despite much practice, little aptitude. Once she had sent a pair to Alex, she felt obliged to furnish a like pair to Charlie. If Alex was her serious soldier boy, Charlie was like a caged wild bird, and she still felt largely responsible for his confinement. The first mud of spring arrived before either pair of mittens was finished.

If Becca failed as a knitter, she redoubled her efforts as correspondent. In all things, the pace seemed to quicken. In the newspapers she noted that only poor weather kept the Union army from moving like a great serpent to throttle the South, and she sat up late to get letters off before her soldier boys were on the move. On February 28 she told Alex:

I have a miserable pen and am sitting in the center of the floor with book in lap and lamp in hand. With Julia having her first son three days ago we have been very busy. I wish Julia did not look so pale.

Alex replied in better humor. Spring was in the air.

We have gained a splendid victory. Manassas is ours without the loss of blood.

Clearly the army was on the move, and in the euphoria of expected victory, Becca's brother Douglas resolved to enlist.

Though Becca's opinion had no weight in his decision, she opposed his joining the army. In her journal she wrote: "It is enough for brother Frank to go."

To Charlie she wrote:

I think Alex is mistaken in saying I gave him a promise of a photograph. He asked for one and I said "Yes, if Mother is willing." Mother like myself does not approve of each young lady giving her pictures to several young gents. I think when the gents are going to war it is all right to leave theirs with the girls but not the opposite way. Now Mother says if I write another word tonight she will pour all my ink away.

Charlie wrote announcing he was bored.

When you got me to sign up for this war Bec I thought I'd have a good scrape not all this squelching about in the mud!!! You won't approve but about our only amusement is liquor which the sutlers bring in. It is awful stuff really with all sorts of names such as "bust skull" and "oil of gladness" "Tangle foot" and "nockum stiff." Of course Alex and the Captain don't approve and the last time to get a little booze past the guards we had to hide it in a canteen which we buried under the floor, taking turns sipping the elixir through a long straw. Yes Bec I can just see you shaking your head, maybe your finger too. But who knows, now that I can call you the innkeeper's daughter.

About the same time a letter from Alex complained:

I suppose it's the boredom and waiting for something to happen but even with the military police out in force, our camp is a hard school of profanity and gambling. Our chaplain calls the army a graveyard for morals. Those who become intoxicated must carry a log on their shoulders. Most do very well for the first hour. Come the second, they begin to look serious, shifting from shoulder to shoulder. By the third, rest assured, the average man is pleading for mercy, though I'm not sure it is a lesson learned for long.

Charlie had his own complaints.

Bec, our regimental band seems to know nothing but "Pop Goes the Weasel." Please forgive me if I never dance to that tune again.

About the incessant lice, he reported:

You can boil your uniform every night, or you can pray.

"Now I lay me down to sleep
while graybacks o'er my body creep
If I should die before I wake
I pray the Lord their jaws to break."

Confidentially, Bec, this doesn't seem to work, either.

Charlie's hopes of finishing the war rose with the first hint of spring weather. In early March of 1862, he wrote to Becca:

We're bound to be heading south soon for our grand and glorious army has overlong shaken the ground around Washington with its tread and drums, and many begin to think it time for us to rattle the windows in Richmond. They say Joe Johnston and his Rebs have pulled out of Centreville. You should have seen the smoke when they set fire to a million pounds of bacon there. So the big excursion party should be off for the "sacred soil" of Dixie any day, and there isn't a man in the old 7th isn't ready for a good muss.

Still the weeks went by, while the Army of the Potomac waited, restless and lice-ridden.

Alex found himself on maneuvers, not the anticipated great push toward Richmond, but a probe south and west, which proved little more than a tourist jaunt.

I have passed through some beautiful scenery and feel well repaid for my tiresome march. In every place we were welcomed by long faces. Harpers Ferry is the prettiest and most romantic place for scenery I ever saw. It is sited on the top in the valley of a large mountain with the Potomac river on one side and the Shenandoah on the other. Its buildings are nearly all brick but entirely deserted, except for a few that were true to the stars and stripes. Co. C is in a large dwelling house, perfect in everything but furniture. It has none of that. This afternoon I made a short visit over to the renowned Jeffersonian rock, where Washington's name is said to have been engraved by himself but it would have taken me years to have read all the names thereon. I took the trouble to engrave my initials. P. S. Becca. At Charleston I visited the place where John Brown was hung and, foolish (like many others) I secured a small piece of the scaffold and of a locust stump where he last stood and made a speech.

On March 21 Becca wrote delightedly that she had received these souvenirs.

With the withdrawal of General Johnston's Confederate army to the southern bank of the Rappahannock River, the goal of the Army of the Potomac became Fortress Monroe, at the tip of the Virginia peninsula. On the eve of the campaign, General McClellan addressed his troops, and Alex, noting that he "liked this kind of general," copied part of the speech for Becca:

"I am to watch over you as a parent over his children; and you know that your general loves you from the depths of his heart. It shall be my care, as it has ever been, to gain success with the least possible loss, but I know that, if it is necessary, you will willingly follow me to your graves for our righteous cause."

The invasion began on March 17 with an armada of sloops, brigs, tugs, steamers, canal boats, and barges, over five hundred in all, with the Seventh Michigan embarking as part of the Third Brigade, Second Division, of General Sumner's Second Corps. Alex wrote to Becca that the scene was majestic, adding:

I suppose you must have heard ere this of our whereabouts but for fear you have not, I will tell you. We had a very pleasant voyage to Fortress Monroe except that on the 2nd night out, the wind blew very hard and a great many experienced the disagreeable feeling of "Sea sickness."

Alex himself had hung over the rail that night, but spared Becca the unsavory details, recounting more objectively:

When we sailed down the Potomac past Mount Vernon the bells of the fleet tolled. What would President Washington have thought of us? We came to anchor at Fortress Monroe and landed there on a sandy beach. Almost the first thing that I saw of interest was the war steamer "Monitor" and never was I more disappointed in the looks of anything. I can scarcely find anything to compare it with unless it is the expression which is going around, "Floating Cheesebox." Nearby the Town of Hampton lay in ruins having been burned by the retreating rebels. And what a sight all those artillery trains going ashore afforded, Zouaves from New York in blue and red and the yellow and blue of the cavalry assembling above the scorched town. Bayonets were flashing like mirrors, tug boats were hooting and sending up plumes of smoke, bands were playing. Becca, it was a sight to see. Once we had pitched our tents we went down to the shoals to gather oysters until a rebel gunboat began firing at us. Nobody was hurt and there was a lot of laughing on shore to see us hopping around like frogs when a snake gets into the pond.

Not until April 4 did the Second Corps go into motion, following General Heintzelman's Third Corps on the road to Yorktown. All the bridges were down, but Alex took pleasure in the gardens, where fruit trees and hyacinths were coming into bloom. When the regiment halted at Big Bethel, Alex began another letter to Becca.

We remained near the ruins of Hampton until a very large force, said to be 200,000 men with 600 cannon were disembarked at the fortress. Then we received marching orders and General McClellan leads us. He passed us twice the last time with hat in hand and cheer after cheer greeted him from many thousands who had not seen him before. It was majestic and his presence gave new energy and resolution to all. Here we passed over entrenchments which the rebs had just evacuated. Slaves were out harvesting castaway shoes and coats. When it was not raining the sun burned down. The road has become a mire and the engineers are busy having young trees cut to put down corduroy roads. We are now encamped on an "Old Revolutionary Battleground" just short of Yorktown. They say General Macgruder commands the rebels there and he has promised to make every house in town a hospital before he will surrender. There! the rebel cannon have begun to fire.

Charlie wrote of the same events:

Dear Friend Bec,

I can't deny it. These rebs have their own sense of humor and one of them drew on the wall of the Big Bethel Hotel, such as it is, the word "Richmond" with a likeness of Old Jeff Davis in a doorway giving the "boot" to General McClellan. Needless to say some of us went to scrub it off and a woman came out with her apron on and pointing at the picture fairly screeched, "You will all drink hot blood before you take Richmond, mark my words." I have to admit I broke out in "gooseflesh" just hearing her.

Charlie had expected a quick march on to Richmond, but the rains set in, swelling muddy streams. Roads turned to gumbo, and every spot of low ground became a swamp. Confederates manned the few crossings on the Warwick River, and instead of outflanking the rebel forces, McClellan set about investing Yorktown, surrounding it with Union troops to prevent any rebels from escaping. He was, after all, an engineer at heart, and had been an observer at the seige of Sevastopol during the Crimean War. In his letter to Becca Charlie explained:

It has rained every day and every day I've dug trenches when it might have been California gold. Oh well, I'm a patriot now. Our work often cut through trenches dug eighty years ago during the Revolution. Is Washington turning in his grave I wonder? We can't have fires at night for fear of sharp shooters but Johnny Reb lights up the sky which I reckon keeps off the mosquitoes and Lord knows what other biting things. Some of the boys are singing "Old Hundred." Our Alex leads the choir and pretty soon, the Hymn spread to the entire army. I do suspect Johnny Reb must have thought the avenging angels of heaven were upon him. I'm not easily impressed Bec, but that

66

was something to hear and it lifted our soggy spirits along with the news that New Orleans has been taken.

On May 3 Alex wrote:

The Rebels are putting up an awful din, shouting and firing off guns. We have over 100 seige cannon in place and nary a one is answering back.

This letter was not completed until six days later, with Alex noting:

When the news of the evacuation of Yorktown first came into camp I hardly knew whether to rejoice or not, but that night when I rested within their works, and saw what they had left, I thanked God from my heart that this was so, for great must have been the slaughter. It seems as if they might defy the world.

The second night we rested within the inner works but were not permitted to go around much as Torpedoes, Cap shells etc. were planted all around and several lives were lost thereby. The next day (5th) we took steamers for this place, where Franklin's division had already landed for the purpose (it is supposed) of cutting them off from Richmond. We had hardly landed when volley after volley of musketry greeted our ears from our pickets. We were quickly in battle time, and the booming cannon soon after began to add to the excitement. We surely expected a general engagement and advanced forward into a large Pine Woods and had scarcely got into position when a Rebel Battery opened fire upon our vessels in the river.

Of his experiences in and around Yorktown, Charlie saw fit to mention a small Confederate cemetery that the Seventh Michigan passed as it marched out of town.

You know, Bec, I can't work up a lot of spleen against these southern boys because they really do show concern, even put up a sign: "Come along Yank, there's room inside for you."

# SEVEN

# Forty Thieves, Hardtack, and Slow Deer

THEY MARCHED OUT OF YORKTOWN an invincible army, all the passing feet leather-shod or bare, muddy legs marching pair on pair, thousands upon thousands. When the sun shone through on the rumbling columns, bayonets gleamed like so many wavering picket fences. Hooves beat like drums as the batteries of bronze napoleons clattered by, the cannoneers clinging to the caissons.

It had begun raining again when Alex heard thunder. "What's that?" he asked, seeing other startled faces. "The rebs," Charlie told him. They had come to a narrow brown stream. Smoke billowed out of the trees and cannonballs crashed louder and deadlier. The field guns had been unlimbered and were blowing fierce smoke rings into the trees. "Make every shot count!" an officer shouted. "Remember each one costs your government eight dollars!"

The heavy air shook with the cannonade. A man just ahead of Alex and Charlie settled down as though he were too tired to proceed. He lay there when the regiment moved on, resting in a puddle that was turning red around him, and Alex, who found the sight awful to behold and whose head turned dizzy, thought, I must have made a mistake; this isn't the way I expected it in Jonesville. They were into the first redoubts east of Williamsburg when the Confederates came on in a wave, Longstreet's men, all veterans, chanting in derision "Bull Run! Bull Run! Bull Run!"

Alex ducked against a tree as a volley let go like chain lightning in the murky light, and a minié ball sped by swelling from E-flat to F, then back down the scale to D. The Seventh was falling back. The whole Federal line crumpled into the woods, where many panicked and fled. One soldier yelled at Alex in passing, "Give 'em hell, boys. I gave them hell long as I could." From the way he was disrobing, it looked as if he meant to give them everything else: gun, hat, coat, cartridge box.

Next, General Kearny's division pounded up to the firing line, with Kearny shouting, "Don't flinch, boys; they're shooting at me, not at you!" and with laughter on their lips the Seventh Michigan plowed ahead again through the mud. Then the whole line stiffened. Alex had been through alarms, occasional picket fire, a skirmish, but this was their first battle. He'd never killed anything much. He had never liked hunting. Charlie'd gotten used to shooting squirrels, though it made him sick at first, but now they were shooting at men. Beyond the muddy stream were rebels, and the shots they fired now might go and kill, though it didn't feel like it. Afterward, neither figured that he had hit anybody, though both took a certain cautious pride in having expended a portion, however minuscule, of the ammunition consumed during the Civil War.

Alex wrote to Becca that night:

Strange why the sounds of war combine to make us think of something glorious, the regiment singing together as one voice, cavalry racketing down a moonlit road.

It had all seemed so right. Someone had told him the regimental band had played throughout. Alex had never heard it. All he remembered hearing were the guns. Now, with the Confederates withdrawing again, they marched across the field, where dead men and horses lay trampled in the mud, the men with their pockets turned out. Alex even saw one looter take a bloody stick of tobacco from a corpse, wash it in a puddle, and begin to chew. Pray God, I never come to that, Becca, he thought. Just as strange, as they went west again, the road led past a trampled corpse whose right hand rose imploringly. Charlie broke ranks, took a piece of hardtack, and pressed it between the stiff fingers. "Poor reb never will make it to California," he said. Then they all marched on.

The rain fell fitfully, and the long column trod the road into a bog, its feet heavy with mud. "I feel like I'm lifting the entire earth with each step," Charlie told Alex, and Alex just looked at him, too tired to reply.

On the 17th Charlie wrote:

Friend Bec,

Seems I owe you a letter. Even greasing my pore old feet with camphor ointment isn't much use but we've plenty of raw bacon, dry bread and enough coffee to swim in. They say we're only one more long march to Richmond so I reckon Johnny Reb's days are numbered and believe me I'm ready to get out of this "war muss" and return to good old jogalong Jonesville.

Alex surveyed the passing scene through the eyes of a country boy. With the rain and warmth, nature had gone wild in one vast competition of growing and flowering. Marching along the south side of the Pamunkey River, he took note of hummingbirds and snakes, the old mansions, and plantation ladies in muslin dresses, surrounded by fearful black children, watching the troops go by. There was a moon, and the land-scape seemed strange and haunting, all green-black and silvery, with long vistas fading off into shadow-land. In the violet light, vapors rose from the swamps, and Alex thought of the river as a snake uncoiling across the map. Finally the regiment halted, and he slumped onto a log, and, amid the insistent drone of mosquitoes, searched for paper and pencil.

Dear Becca,

It isn't far to Richmond now. I believe they call this place Fair Oaks and indeed vast oaks spread above us. I hate to say it but our men are using this country awfully rough and all animals such as chickens and hogs have vanished. The white women here abouts will not speak to us and prefer pulling their hats down over their eyes but the slaves are friendly and enterprising, selling us what food they can spare including spring cabbage greens which they call "collards." We camped near the White House Plantation yesterday which is said to belong to the Confederate General Robert E. Lee. Some of the boys were talking about burning it down. I hope not as it is a pretty place.

Becca, we can hear the rebel sentries talking or singing and at night I can see the quick flare as they cup their hands to a pipe. I feel we'll have a scrape soon and if the future is at best uncertain, we can't let it scare us and I do feel before summer is truly here I will be posting letters home to you from Richmond.

When Charlie wrote, it was to complain about food, particularly the salt beef, or "Junk," which was scarcely fit to eat, and most of which they had dumped out on the ground. He wrote:

It is fat for the most part, and what I took for a bit of lean turned out to be nothing but rust off the pan. Not to say the hard tack is any better. I was chewing on one of those blessed biscuits and what do you suppose, I bit through something soft. A worm, you say? Well Bec not so, it was a ten penny nail. Consequently the more enterprising among us, friend Alex not included, have banded together into what some are calling "The Forty Thieves," and in consequence we are eating commendably again. The hogs that run wild in the woods round about are known to us as "slow deer" while a flock of Secesh geese that had the affrontery to hiss at Old Glory were executed on the spot. Then Capt. Vrooman caught us on the way back with those traitor geese slung from our rifles and he bellowed, "I want you gentlemen to understand I'm not punishing you for stealing but for getting caught at it." He didn't do it, though, not when he got wind that his own cook was preparing goose liver for his supper.

My health is still bully, never better and Capt. Vrooman says we'll be home by mid summer, in which case we will have a gay old time. If not let us fight until Secession is buried so deep that not even the Devil himself can lift it from the grave.

For all this self-assurance, Charlie's next letter, and it followed within days, expressed doubts.

Friend Bec,

I feel a great battle looms, though many do say the rebels want to keep us in these Chickahominy marshes until the summer fever fairly melts the army away. Better to fight, say I, and yet Bec I do wonder at times if I am made of such metal as can stand the test. Why do I expect a battle? you may well ask, because the company today drew a requisition of shoes. So a march seems certain, and after a march comes a battle, though the undersigned feels he will probably live on in the hearts of his comrades or somewhere at any rate and he does not expect to lose more than two or three legs and an arm or so in the service of his country, but the thing is, a fool part of him doesn't want to look bad. He doesn't want to run off.

Alex says, not to worry, the company will do fine. And I am a good shot. I mean you're not likely to miss a man when you're used to squirrels and rabbits, but am I brave, Bec? I sometimes suspect that courage is nothing more than the greater fear of being thought a coward. Capt. Vrooman expects us to show disregard of danger but I'm not sure I can be that deceitful. Bec, how can you tell a dead man he died an heroic death? I have seen dead men and some look asleep and some look shocked or puzzled. Most just stare, but you can ask questions 'til you're blue in the face. Was it worth it? or would you run away the next time? but I've seldom heard of a better way to avoid danger than running away.

Well here comes the rain again and these words will be doing what I can't, run, if I don't find cover. Is it raining in Jonesville? Can it be raining in California, I hardly think so.

With this, Charlie ran for shelter as the rain became a drumming downpour.

He was accustomed by now to sleeping in a soaking-wet uniform, and slept soundly that night of May 30, 1862. He woke to the sound of bird song and smiled at the dream memory of promising never to drink, curse, or gamble. Lightning had killed two men in a tent during the night, but Charlie had not heard the commotion. Now it was that quiet time when dew formed before the dawn. There was no more peaceful time, the grayness in the air seeming to empty the world. For a moment, there was no more camp, no more war. Then the sun bore red through the fog, an invisible sun illuminating the landscape. Opaque screens of low mist shifted, withdrew, closed. Charlie noted that the trees seemed to weep, that the river was near flood, that he was hungry, that it was the last day of May. Soldiers around him began snapping percussion caps to dry the tubes of their rifles.

The Seventh Michigan Regiment awoke slowly, quietly. For all that, Charlie had a feeling of impending disaster. "The light's strange," he said to Alex, who sat on a log, yawning. "Sort of yellow." Alex agreed. Little spirals of mist rose from the river like smoke rings from a giant's pipe. Alex shivered and said, "Nice morning for a hanging."

A distant bugle uttered a sharp, strident stammer. Presently the post arrived. Both Charlie and Alex had letters to mail, and an irritated voice wanted to know if they were the ration detail for the Twenty-third Ohio. The bugle presently announced breakfast with "Peas on a Trencher."

"Too quiet by half," Alex said. They were eating with other boys from Jonesville when Charlie nudged Alex as an officer with a full white beard rode up. "That's Bull Sumner," he said. The general was speaking to Captain Vrooman. Then he turned to the Jonesville boys. "How do you gentlemen feel?" he asked. "Is there anything going to stop you from going to Richmond?" His voice was rich and booming, and they yelled back, "Hell no, general!"

"I get uneasy when generals see fit to speak to me," Charlie said, and Alex agreed.

Their mood deepened when General McClellan also put in an appearance. He stood in his stirrups, shouting, "Soldiers of the Potomac, I have filled at least a part of my promise to you. You are now face to face with the enemy before his capital. The final and decisive battle is at hand. May I count on you, as I hope you will depend on me?" Again they shouted "Yes!" before he rode off down the line.

"Now I know we're in for trouble," Charlie observed.

Horses rumbled past, all lathered, throwing up a thin soup

of mud. Behind them, more like red-striped dummies nailed in place than like men, the crews jolted with the ammunition wagons. Finally came the lunging brass field guns. Bugles began braying their brazen commands, "Ta-ta-tatata." The colonel tried to tell his men this was the opening of the ball, the moment they had so eagerly awaited, but the pace of things now outstripped words. Their regimental colors were uncased. Red battle flags drooped from the staffs. The Seventh Michigan reached for cartridge boxes and caps, not waiting for the order to load. A rapid pulse beat in Alex's forehead. Strange, he thought, how war made one feel so alive. He noticed that Charlie's cheeks stood out over clenched jaws, holding his fear in check as a rider commands a panicky horse.

Not until one in the afternoon did they hear thunder again, in dry crescendo, forecasting ruin instead of rain. "They're coming," Charlie said, and Alex nodded back. The captain was shouting at them, shrill as a scolding squirrel, to hold their fire. Too late, Alex thought; the only escape left was the flight of his eyes back through the trees. The long-anticipated big battle was now.

# EIGHT

# *Fair Oaks*

REBECCA CASE COUNTED THE DAY FORTUNATE INDEED when she heard from both her beaux, and such was the third day of June 1862. The letters arrived with her father, who bore as well a copy of the *Jonesville Weekly Independent*, which sang in large headlines, COSTLY VICTORY. BATTLE RAGES AT FAIR OAKS. THE JONESVILLE COMPANY ENGAGED.

Though Becca liked to think of herself as psychic, she had felt no premonition that Friday, when she had stayed home from school, as the weather was warm and her father was down with Michigan fever. After bringing him tea, she attended "a special service for our boys" at the Presbyterian church, confiding in her journal that the new preacher seemed "dry as a stick." Then came the newspaper account and Charlie's letter telling of the Seventh's first real fight, along the curving banks of the Chickahominy, all the Jonesville boys together, their red battle flag slanting forward, high as their hearts.

Charlie had whistled to appear calm at first, while behind the regiment, the field guns opened up, pounding themselves hub-deep into the mud. Skirmishers ran ducking and firing through the trees. Then the gray men had come on through the whispering thickets, and he'd heard the terrible rip and tear of musketry volleys and seen the rolling wall of smoke pricked out with blades of fire. The Federal troops held off Johnston's veterans and raised a shrill cheer of victory, only to have it die away with the cry, "Here they come again!"

The captain shouted, "Load and fire! Load and fire!"

Again the Confederates fell back, only to come on a third, then a fourth time, with the Jonesville boys being pressed into the swamp. "Seventh Michigan, rally here!" Captain Vrooman's usually deep and commanding voice sounded as though it issued from the lips of a girl, and all that held Charlie in place, he decided later, was dread of being shamed before the folks back home. He saw Alex next to a pine trunk, crouched and firing, and took his place with his friend. Around them rushed strange crowds. On either side was the gleam of bayonets, then the long ragged flash of fire, and they clung to the tree as a kind of life raft in a savage sea, while high above the storm, and glimpsed occasionally through the smoke, Professor Lowe's observation balloon rode serene.

While others fell back, the two clung to their tree, loading and firing, as afternoon gave way to evening and the musketry blazed in the thickets. With complete darkness, the fighting broke off. Then the surgeons appeared, their lamps bobbing like glowworms in the dark. Alex and Charlie clung to their battle-gnawed trunk, too weary to move until Captain Vrooman came up, his left arm in a sling. "I've never seen men behave better," he said. "You two anchored the company, and the Jonesville boys anchored the entire line. Rest assured, the colonel will hear about this. Good work, boys."

Alex and Charlie smiled weakly back. Surely, only terror had frozen them there. "What do you think of that?" Alex asked. Then Charlie began to laugh. Presently they were both giddy with laughter, heroes of the Seventh Michigan.

With only a little swamp water that night to slake their thirst, they slept where they had fought. Toward dawn, the sky looked like dirty milk. Mist lay everywhere. Awakening, they gazed at each other like strangers, their eyes red with fatigue and gunpowder irritation, cheeks flecked with powder and dried mud, singed from the flash of priming, clothes torn and filthy, with even a spattering of blood, though they'd received no wounds.

"Well, it's good to know what a certified hero looks like," Charlie observed. "I'd never have guessed."

Painfully, dirty water was boiled, and Alex found a bag of coffee and sugar mixed. Charlie produced a small tin of beans, trading it off for a token of salt pork, saying, "Looks more like mule to me," but they were glad of what they had, scarcely swallowing it before, down the line, firing began.

It was seven o'clock in the morning, and reinforcements were coming up. The Confederates showed no signs of budging. Alex and Charlie sought out their faithful tree, but not before Zum-cats, as the minié balls were called, whistled and cracked above, bringing down twigs and fluttering leaves. "Hold out a bushel basket," Charlie observed, "and we'll fill it up with bullets in no time."

Mist and smoke hung like curtains of dingy wool, shredding away little by little as the sunlight probed through, revealing small, monstrous pictures of what war at close quarters could do, pictures that bit into the brain forever.

Alex and Charlie were dead tired and low on ammunition when the men behind them began cheering. General Sumner was riding up with fresh troops. The only bad part of going forward was leaving their tree, which by this time had the properties of a near-magical guardian. The advance took them across a log bridge upon which floodwater rippled. An engineer assured General Sumner that to cross was suicidal. Still, the bearded old man replied, "Impossible? Sir, I tell you I can cross. I am ordered." And so they went over, with the weight of the tramping men seeming to anchor the bridge.

They were on the far bank when Charlie noticed Alex hunched over, his left hand clasped to his thigh. "What's wrong?" he asked, to which Alex replied through clenched teeth, "I think they got me."

There had been only stray firing at the time, but a flurry thereafter, as they retook the parcel of field, swamp, and scrub forest where they had begun fighting the day before. There the battle of Fair Oaks ended, and for Alex, who had limped along, firing, even cheering weakly with the others, it was the end of the campaign.

"I'm feeling a mite shaky," Alex admitted when all about him had begun to swim and lose focus. Charlie had to help him to the lee side of a small barn, into which an occasional minié ball drove with the impact of a hammer. Wounded from both sides sought shelter there, and a Georgia private with his shirt tied around his head as a bandage kept asking, "Oh, Lord, why'd you come down here to fight us? We'd never a come up there. We'd never . . ." Alex was not up to a debate, but when a neighbor began to sing "Somebody's Darling," he joined in. Why not? They were all of them some- body's darling. He hoped so, anyway. It would be awful if nobody cared.

Not until the second day of turmoil gave way to evening sounds was the magnitude of Alex's wound revealed when Charlie applied a dampened handkerchief. "You've got a mi- nié ball in there," Charlie observed. "I don't know how you kept going. Well . . ." Only then did he notice that his friend had fainted. He assured himself that Alex was still breathing, stood up, and took a deep, shuddering breath of his own. "We'll need a stretcher from here on." Many of the litter bearers, dragooned musicians for the most part, had fled the fight, and it was well after dark before Alex was carried to the rear and Charlie could surrender to his own exhaustion.

In the morning, the two hostile armies licked their wounds, and Charlie wrote:

Old friend Bec,

We have been in a considerable fight. As you have probably heard by now, Alex was hit.

She had in fact seen a newspaper account on Saturday, June 7, which she translated into her diary. "Read in today's paper that Alex was slightly wounded in the battle of Fair Oaks last Sunday while fighting with many other brave ones in the glorious cause. Perhaps it may be the means of his speedy return. If so, and as the wound is slight, I am almost glad it happened." She was unprepared for the balance of Charlie's letter, which said:

I hope very much that he does not lose his leg, for his sake and for mine, not just because he is a best friend but because I fear he would have a great advantage over me where your sympathies are concerned.

After the newspaper account, such an ominous report came as a shock to Becca, filling her with a riot of conflicting feelings: distress, the obvious sympathy and concern that Charlie had mentioned, overlaid by the image of herself wed to a cripple.

I cannot be so selfish, I can't be, she thought, but she dreamed that night of old Mr. Sibley, veteran of the War of 1812, creaking about Brooklyn on a little cart. Both of his legs were gone at the knees, and when they had buried him, with a speech by the mayor, the coffin had been so terribly short.

# NINE

## Under the Knife

ON JUNE 12, having heard that Alex was in a New York hospital, Becca wrote him a letter in care of her sister in Brooklyn, Sarah Case Bergen. Becca hoped, in rather stilted fashion, that he was not in pain, that while in New York he might visit her sister, and that he would soon be home to recuperate. She did not know whether he still had both legs, and she dared not ask.

Two days later, long before her letter reached New York, Alex returned to Jonesville by train. He had grown whiskers, she was told, and was too exhausted by the trip for visitors. On June 19, when the Jonesville paper was recounting the costs of Fair Oaks ("It is with extreme regret that we have to report the loss to this regiment, in killed and wounded, of from 95 to 100, of which 14 were killed"), Becca was requested to pay her first visit. Alex was asleep when she entered the room, and within the space of a heartbeat she saw that he had been shaved clean and that both feet pushed the thin blanket upward. A second heartbeat told her that he was terribly pale and feverish.

Becca waited patiently for Alex to awaken, then said, with forced brightness, "Thanks to goodness, you're all well."

"All well?" He looked at the ceiling, not at her. "Yes, I suppose, for now."

What did he mean by that? She did not want to ask, but inquired instead, "Did they treat you well, the doctors and all?"

"Well as anyone else," he replied. "Let's not reflect on that, not now."

Becca had her questions to hide. Alex had answers he did not want to give. So at that first meeting both became pleasant, yet cautious, actors with things to conceal—she out of fear, he because he could never tell how it had really been.

Those first days, the thunder of battle had suddenly concentrated in his leg a core of pain, which, if nothing else, did remind Alex he was not dead. In fact the pain had been muted, though his leg looked as though it had been chewed by wolves.

For a while he had kept up, loading and firing, screaming, wielding his rifle against a thing that broke, feeling, as the advance moved forward, that he skimmed the earth. When he finally lay down in yesterday's battle field, Alex had thought he was still on his feet, walking forward. Then his hands were red from where he had pressed them against his leg, and in that blasted world, he was almost grateful that he was still alive enough to bleed.

That night of June 1, as Alex had waited, in and out of consciousness, a rebel casualty lay beside him, panting heavily, like a fish cast up on the shore. The man's glassy eyes had protruded. Clearly he did not know that he still lived. Alex had felt kinship for this stranger, whom, as a healthy enemy, he might have detested. "He's somebody's darling," he kept thinking distractedly. "He must be somebody's darling." Presently a rose-colored beard overlaid the rebel's short black one, and Alex had made a point of looking the other way.

He did not mind the rain that had begun to fall slowly. Nothing seemed to matter, and he drifted in and out of consciousness until Charlie roused him with, "Old friend, it's time to go." Charlie had rounded up a pair of litter bearers. Feebly, Alex had protested. Better to die here of a rebel bullet than from Union quacks. But Charlie had given him a drink of water for his raging thirst and packed him off to a forward aid station, where all the attention he received in the next twenty-four hours was a shot of whiskey and some damp straw beneath him. Flies had buzzed up like plucked violin strings when he'd been moved onto a canvas stretcher, stiff with dried blood, and carried joltingly to a wagon, which creaked down two miles of bumpy road to a field hospital at Savage's Station.

There the ground had been wet, as were the straw upon it and the blanket with which he was covered and left to wait. Dimly, Alex heard the screams of men under the knife as he lay there waiting, telling himself that when he had gathered sufficient strength, he would walk back and surprise Charlie and the boys. He had to shut his eyes to fight the dizziness and nausea, and finally he realized that time had passed and the sun had slid around in the sky.

Good Lord, he'd thought, I might have woken up dead. I can't lie here. Nobody dies of a smashed leg. Still he did not move, until finally, with a great effort, he made it over onto one elbow. Then he saw that his leg was oozing again, and he managed with his last strength to scrape up a handful of mud and plaster it over the wound. He fell back, exhausted, and waited, in and out of consciousness, for the surgeons. Were they leaving him to die in peace? That thought suddenly became so horrible that Alex had begun to cry out, which had brought another swallow of raw whiskey and an agonizing lifting and carrying into a long tent that was the nearest thing to a vision of hell that Alex would ever experience.

In the light of guttering candles and smoking kerosene lamps, Alex beheld a satanic scene: surgeons in blood-spattered aprons, their wounded patients, cast upon doors that had become operating tables, calling weakly for water, for Mother, praying, cursing, dying, while severed feet, arms, legs, hands were cast into corners. Chloroform had run out by the time Alex received attention. Over him the surgeons leaned close. There were tiny spots of blood on the spectacles of one doctor. The filthy rags of Alex's trousers were cut away. A bucket of water, pinkly tinted, had sloshed the mud from his leg, which one of the surgeons explored with bare fingers while a roaring and a flaming rose inside Alex and a dull grunt soared into a scream. He tried to clasp his hands to his ears, impossible, as his hands were bound fast, and useless, since the cry had come from his own cracked lips. Finally the world whirled and slipped and blacked out as though he had stared too long at the sun. When he wakened, it was but painful seconds later, and the surgeon with the spectacles was holding up a misshapen minié ball, which seemed far too small for the dark puncture in his thigh from which it had been extracted.

"I expect you'll survive," the surgeon said, wiping his perspiring forehead with the back of his hand. "You may even walk again on both legs." Then this vision faded into a roaring darkness.

A dawn ray knifed through the tent flap and beset Alex's eyes. He groaned, tried to roll over, and awoke. At first he thought he heard church bells, and imagined the Jonesville girls in blue-and-white dresses, all scrubbed and bonneted for Sunday service. "Oh, Becca," he said, but the voice that replied was Charlie's voice.

"I might have known," it said. "Well, I guess you're on the mend." Waking, Alex had seen the pleasure in Charlie's eyes and felt the uncommon friendship in his own. "Look after that leg, and you may just keep it awhile." Outside it rained again. The drops fell like a curtain of splintered glass. Charlie had walked the two miles to the hospital and was soaked to the skin. He hadn't seemed to notice. "You know, you could be a lot worse off," he said seriously. "I just overheard a surgeon speaking to another wounded soldier. He was saying, 'Poor fellow, I can't help you. Your head's been shot off.' Then the soldier said, 'Doesn't matter a bit. I'm General Sumner and I don't need one.' Seriously, Alex, I envy you. You'll be heading home today, I expect. Now don't take advantage of Becca, you hear?"

Going home. It had seemed worth the dull pain, but Alex had not left that day or the next, for Confederate general Stuart, with his red beard and feathered plumes, had come riding with twelve hundred dragoons around the Union Army. They had stopped briefly at the field hospital. With the grace of a cavalier, Stuart had taken only those medicines the doctors could spare, but the rails to the rear were blocked, telegraph wires were cut, and no wounded patients were moved until long after the enemy had pounded south and then back to Richmond.

When Alex was moved, the flies had had time to work on his wound. He was feverish again by the time he went slowly, on a clattering flatcar, down the Richmond and York River Line to White House landing. Flatboats took the wounded from there, down the meandering Pamunkey River, to the wider York, with transfer at last to a hospital ship, the *Daniel Webster*, bound for Washington City. Drifting in and out of consciousness, Alex kept wondering if the sweet smell of decomposition came from his leg or from all those others.

Nurses were aboard the ship, and he learned later he had been tended by Eliza Howland, whose uncle was the president of Yale College. She had brought him food and changed his bandage, saying, "The doctor had best have a look at this," and he had called her Becca and never wanted her to leave his side.

In Washington, Julia Wheelock of the Michigan Soldiers' Relief Association took charge, provided food and blankets, agreed in whispers with a doctor that the leg looked bad, but, with the overcrowding, decided he stood a better chance in New York, where Alex's papers indicated he had relatives. So Alex spent only three hot, feverish days in a Washington "hospital" that was really a barracks, before being carried aboard a swaying hospital car, New York bound. Another week, and a debate among surgeons as to whether his leg should be removed on the spot, and he was packed off to Jonesville. Let his family and the hometown quack decide.

This group of experts, as Becca was to discover on leaving Alex's bedside, had come to no firm decision. The doctor, good-hearted, but in terms of surgical practice naive, maintained the leg should come off before the infection spread. On the other hand, he confessed to having amputated a leg only once, with the patient expiring from shock on the spot. Alex's mother suggested leaving it up to God, to which Dr. Brennan responded with skeptical grunts. Clearly, he questioned this approach, then turned to a startled Becca for her opinion, leaning toward her as though beseeching sympathy.

"Will he die if he keeps his leg?" she asked.

"Quite possibly," the doctor replied, hands clasped together. "Quite possibly, though he's making a remarkable fight."

"I should hope so," Becca answered. "It can't be very nice being dead, especially when you're young." For an instant she beheld the image of a deformed child, and still she said it. "I know Alex would hate being a cripple."

Curious how that seemed to decide things. The doctor agreed they could wait and see, and when Alex was strong enough to ask her opinion a second time, Becca replied, as if appealing to someone older and stronger than herself, that it was his decision to make.

"If I'm to die, I want to go to the promised land with all my limbs attached," he said. This of course left open the question of when, but Becca replied with clear relief, "I knew you'd say that." The next time she called, Alex showed her a pistol hidden under his pillow, explaining, "Don't worry, nobody but God gets this leg."

Julia, who had not visited Alex, contributed her usual note of comfort. "If you ask me, Bec, it's best to be prepared for the worst. Just assume he's not going out the door alive, then—" At this Becca turned her back on her sister-in-law, her skirt swirling.

The next day, Alex seemed much better, and they talked of the Jonesville volunteers, especially of Charlie Gregory, who had written Alex from New Bridge, Virginia, on June 21.

Alex,

I expect by now you're doing cartwheels with the laugh on all of us. Should anyone inquire after me, tell them Greg's still part of the Pot-o-mac army but not for long. Tell them—well, I'll be hanged if I care what you tell them so long as you tell it bad enough. Alex, the Jonesville people consider me a hard pit, and I'm getting that way, and with any luck we will be home come autumn at which point you will hear me shout "Let the Army and the war go to the devil." I am heartily sick of it and would give a hundred dollars if I was at home today. You can bet when that happens they won't get me back here again.

Yes, I long for the time when our faces shall be aimed towards old Michigan and you and I can turn Jonesville upside down, girls and all. Will we? or will we not? And by the way, give my love to the innkeeper's daughter.

"You know, I rather blame myself for his joining up," Becca admitted after Alex had read her a slightly censored version of Charlie's letter.

"Oh?"

"I even used you as a good example."

This seemed quite proper to Alex. "Don't fret over friend Gregory. He's hale as an autumn apple. I don't believe there's a bullet been made that could hurt our Charlie."

Indeed, throughout the balance of the Peninsula campaign, Charlie thrived, but the Army of the Potomac did not. Though Fair Oaks had been a standoff, its consequences were profound. Confederate General Johnston had been wounded there, placing his army under new command, while Union General McClellan, too compassionate perhaps for a field general, remained appalled at the casualties and set about the taking of Richmond by slow seige.

General Robert E. Lee, the Army of Northern Virginia's new leader, had no intention of abiding by his opponent's design, and struck quickly at Mechanicsville, Gaines' Mill, Savage's Station, and Frayser's Farm. The Yankees acquitted themselves well enough where respective casualties were concerned, and yet McClellan, always claiming he was outnumbered, retreated—"changed base" in his own words. After winning most of the fights on paper, he managed to lose the campaign, not through want of courage, but because his apprehension of failure, and consequent lack of daring, doomed him to fail.

On July 1 Union cannon, ranked hub-to-hub, cut the advancing Confederate ranks to pieces. A more sanguine commander might have advanced victoriously down Malvern Hill through the dead and wounded all the way to Richmond, but a dejected McClellan, looking for the protection of his forces, withdrew yet again. Of all this Charlie Gregory was a part, and when he had time, he wrote to both Becca and Alex of his disappointment. He still loved McClellan—most of the army did to the end—but something was wrong.

By the time Charlie arrived back in Washington in late summer, he was even more homesick and weary of soldiering.

Bec, we're in the right, God knows, but we're losing all the same. I guess it's only in songs and history books that the right always triumphs. Rest assured, if I am granted a Christmas leave, the Army of the Potomac won't see this lad again.

"Amen to that," Becca wrote in her diary. She was simply tired of responsibility: responsibility for Alex's leg—he was still bedridden; sometimes, when his fever rose, despaired of—and responsibility for Charlie, too. Let the rebels go their way. Let the slaves remain slaves forever, so long as her two beaux were safe at home and able to renew their friendly rivalry for her hand, which some day she felt sure she would give to one or the other.

TEN

# Home for the Holidays

THOUGH THE WEATHER REMAINED FIERCELY HOT in Jonesville, the summer of 1862 moved toward autumn. Evenings
brought distant thunder that seldom meant rain, and Becca
often rode alone in the moonlight. Sometimes she went as far
as Pulaski to visit Douglas and Julia, and to help with their
baby which Julia insisted was more than she could handle.
With another on the way Douglas no longer spoke of joining
the regiment. The rest of Becca's free time was spent at Alex's
bedside, and the more she visited him, the more she felt she
sat with a stranger. Yet, was the stranger her old self, or
Alex, who looked so pale and tired? Becca could not decide.
Sometimes Alex was feverish and as waxen as a tallow candle.
Then his skin had a pewter sheen and Becca would say, "Oh,
your poor leg, does it hurt?" She was not afraid of the clean
white bandage, but the smell—the strong, sweet, sickening
scent of a wound that refused to heal—made Becca want to
flee outside.

Sometimes Becca felt Alex was better, at others that he
might lose the leg or die. They did not discuss it. They spoke
little. Becca read aloud sometimes. Mostly it seemed enough

her simply being there. When Alex spoke, his voice was as frail and crinkly as tissue paper, but his pain seemed lost in her nearness. There was no despair in him. He had no talent in that regard, and when Becca asked, "How do you feel, really?" he replied, smiling, "Well, fine, for anyone who'd been given up for dead. Just suppose I were dead now, in the very same bed where I was born. Now that would be a curiosity."

"We can't have you talking like that."

"Well, I reckon I won't die for a while yet."

Old Dr. Brennan on his regular rounds brought laudanum for pain, which Alex refused, and told his patient that he was doing just fine. Downstairs he gave Alex's mother a soothing syrup for the lingering cough she had developed, warned her of possible complications beyond the resources of his medicine, and speculated on the likelihood of Alex ever descending the stairs again on his own two feet. The days at Alex's house seemed to Becca like endless Sundays, with folks sitting around waiting for something to happen.

On August 10 a depressed Becca recorded in her journal, "I've just been to call on Alex. The poor fellow is much worse, and his wound must be very painful, though he doesn't say so. The doctor almost despairs of his life now, and it is greatly feared that his leg must be amputated." But the next day Alex improved. His temperature fell, then rose again as the days of August and most of September vanished from the calendar.

Very often Becca feared that Alex clung to his leg on her account. Almost against her will, she offered to dress the wound, but he declined, saying, "It's ugly." There was more to it. The wound was a confession of weakness. Becca felt helpless yet responsible, and the more at fault she deemed herself, the more Becca attended her friend. Never once could she admit that she feared the prospect of marriage to a cripple nearly as much as she feared his death. If only she and Charlie had gone off to California long ago.

Charlie wrote them regularly from Virginia, then Washington.

I am glad our Alex has got home where he can have good care for in these army hospitals it is ten chances to one against a wounded man getting out alive.

Of the soldier's life Charlie complained constantly, though with a sense of humor.

If boredom could kill there wouldn't be a man alive in the 7th. We call the company cook our dog robber and we have new words to go with the mess call.

Soupy, soupy, soupy
without any bean,
Porky, porky, porky,
without any lean
Coffee, coffee, coffee
without any cream.

I count the days until my enlistment is up. Rest assured of that, Bec.

Yet, as the days of Charlie's enlistment diminished, his homesickness grew, and he wrote:

This morning was Sunday and the bells must have jangled for service back home. I can just see you and all the other girls riding to church in your white summer dresses. Well, I've been lucky so far and if I make it through the next muss which I reckon will be pretty soon, I'll tell you one thing Bec, I'd be a

fool not to get out when I have the chance. As you know, I
never much believed in war, but if you ask me there won't be
running away next time. We've seen the elephant and most of
us just want to get this business over and done with.

That was written toward mid-September. The Army of the
Potomac was marching at the time toward the Maryland town
of Sharpsburg and a stream nearby, of no great account,
named Antietam Creek.

After the ignominious campaign in Virginia a large portion
of the Army of the Potomac had joined the newly formed
Army of Virginia, commanded by General John Pope, only to
suffer blundering defeat at the Second Battle of Bull Run.
Now George McClellan, that dapper horseman, the general
who said of his army, "We are wedded and should not be
separated," was back in complete command. Nevertheless,
he led the army he loved so much through the bloodiest day
the Western Hemisphere has ever known. It was McClellan's
last battle. Over half of Charlie's regiment was disabled that
day, but Charlie again emerged without a scratch. He reported to Becca:

Antietam was a slaughterhouse. Colonel Baxter's brother-in-
law was killed. How his wife and children will mourn.

Colonel Baxter was at first also listed among the dead, but
turned up in Jonesville the next month, grievously wounded.
He healed so rapidly that November found him returning to
the regiment.

Charlie's letters contained rumors and conjectures: that Lee
had been stopped, if not defeated, that President Lincoln
would proclaim freedom for the slaves. Charlie was among

95

the few who fought to free the slaves, but not because he knew and loved the blacks, so much as because he could not abide bondage of any kind. He wrote:

> Slavery must die, and Bec, though you know I am not a reverential sort, if Dixie insists on being buried in the same grave, I shall see in it naught but the hand of God.

Lincoln's Emancipation Proclamation was already featured in the Jonesville newspaper when Charlie's letter arrived. By this time, the summer had cooled and the maples had exploded into rainbow tints, not colors, but more like burning lamps, as though the leaves had absorbed the summer sun only to give it back reluctantly. Alex had tossed through his last crisis and had begun taking short walks, moving at first with the stiff lurch of a swinging corpse. Just being out of doors seemed to revive his spirits, and despite the haunted pallor of his face, Becca sensed in him a new repose. "You look just fine," she lied, and day by day their walks grew longer, until so many leaves had fallen that the trees seemed to have turned upside down, their roots grasping for the sky in order to plant themselves there. "Presently, I may have to choose between a discharge or a long furlough, Becca," Alex said one day in November. "I hope you'll think about it, and give me your advice."

"Would you listen to me?" she asked skeptically.

"You know I would, when the time comes."

Days hurtled on toward the holiday season. Charlie wrote:

> Six weeks and I'm a free man. Don't expect we'll have any fighting meanwhile, though the army has a new commander, Ambrose Burnside. I see in a recent issue of the Independent that your father's horse, Frank Moscow, won the harvest trot.

My congratulations. Also that Tom Thumb paid a visit to Jonesville. I hope you saw him, Bec.

She had, having attended the celebrated midget's first performance with Alex, and now a signed photograph of Thumb and his wife resided in her journal, in which Becca recorded on November 29, "Thanksgiving today. I celebrated by partaking of a little turkey, boiled onions, mashed potatoes, cranberry sauce, mince pie, etc."

Meanwhile, General Burnside moved his grumbling army south, down muddy roads and over swollen rivers, until the pontoons required to cross the Rappahannock went astray. While Burnside awaited them impatiently, the Army of Northern Virginia had ample time to dig in on the facing slopes, called Maryes Heights, just above the town of Fredericksburg. By November 25, when the pontoons finally arrived, it was too late to cross there unopposed. For over two weeks, the red eyes of hostile camp fires winked at each other. December 12 dawned sunny and mild. Burnside, after pondering the merits of a dash upriver in order to outflank the foe, decided the only real surprise would be to cross directly under the Confederate guns. This was achieved with scant opposition.

Fredericksburg, much reduced by bombardment, was taken. It remained until the following day, one of cold, heavy fog, to contest the Confederate lines above the town. Federal cannon opened fire from Stafford Heights. The sky cleared, and the Army of the Potomac, with the river at its back, lined up beneath its flapping flags. Among the first to move forward was the Seventh Michigan, with the Nineteenth and Twentieth Massachusetts standing in support. There was a tincture of autumn gold in the air as the ranks advanced. Then the earth began to tremble as the Confederate guns opened fire and men in blue began lying down. The Union troops tried

97

all day to throw the rebels back. Rich reds and purples of sunset mingled with the grimy smoke of the burning town, moving always toward Maryes Heights, which was lit as if by sheet lightning, so steady was the fire that tormented it. That night when the aurora borealis flickered in the sky, the Confederates took it as a sign that God was celebrating.

The *Jonesville Weekly Independent* reported this fiasco, how on the morning of December 14 nine hundred dead lay gleaming nakedly in the cold dawn light before the stone wall of Maryes Heights, stripped of everything from the shoes on their feet to the caps on their heads by the enemy, who wore little more than rags. From Charlie there was a long silence, until an envelope dully spotted with mold, as if from beyond the grave, arrived.

> Our file leader was killed in the first volley. Though I stood beside the colors which were completely hit, I remained unhurt. Even Colonel Henry Baxter was hit. The Colonel is not well liked in some quarters and I heard that he was in Hell pumping thunder at three cents a clap, but it isn't so. He is wounded only and swears he will return to the regiment. Well, yours truly will be long gone by then. The brave are not alone in being killed but surely they have the best chance of it. No more for me. I've used up more luck than one man deserves.

Charlie wrote this in a cow shed, where he and several others had sheltered from the cold rain, and thought of the things he could, but would not, write to Becca. No more friends in pain, no more stupid generals who could only win battles when the enemy general was stupider—which wasn't likely when the rebs were led by Lee and Jackson.

No more watching towns torn apart. Fredericksburg had been a pretty little place when they arrived, but they had bombed it and burned it and the boys had looted every house there, some of them strutting around in ladies' dresses for no good reason. What happened to all those knights in shining armor, who now catcalled filthy words at the old grandmothers shuffling home to their burned-out cellars? If this is civil war, he thought, spare me an uncivil one. Charlie wrote:

It's all rain and mud down here. No dignified Presbyterian drizzle but an all out Baptist downpour, and the army is pretty glum about it. Not even the healthy ones like myself cheer "Old Burny" when he rides by. A good many heed the sick call, which goes

Are you all dead?
Are you all dead?
No, thank the Lord
there's a few left yet.

Kidding aside, Bec, we have all of us seen the elephant and weary of soldiering. All I ask is home for Christmas. Meanwhile, give my love to Alexander Aberdeen, but not too much of your own.

After five months, most of them spent in bed, Alex was up and around all of every day, and, though still using a cane, the December walks he took with Becca were becoming long ones.

"You're wearing me out, Alex, with all this tramping about," she complained with pleasure. But the Michigan weather was fine. Under a dome of cobalt blue, little clouds melted away like snowflakes in the radiant sky. There was no place for sorrow or worry in this frost-glittering world that seemed newborn. The frost took a footprint, and there was a particular delight in walking upon unmarked frost, even more upon the first skim of snow.

"I'll be fit for service before long," Alex observed. He did not seem to relish the thought.

"You're still limping," she protested.

"I may always," he admitted, leaning to one side, straightening up, leaning to the other. "At first it felt awkward, like trying out stilts." His right hand fiercely gripped the head of his father's cane. When Becca offered her shoulder, Alex did not refuse. "Look at it this way," Alex joked, "there's just enough lead in my body to give me weight. If I go back, who knows, they may insist I become an officer."

"I wish the war was over," Becca replied with sharp impatience. "I'm sick of it. How long can it last?"

With their last domestic helper gone off to work at Gardiner's woolen mill, chores kept Becca at home. On December 20 this meant assisting her father in butchering the Christmas hog, a bloody business from which Becca looked away when she could. The sausage making seemed to go on forever, and she was exhausted. She was washing up in the kitchen, above her elbows in a pan of steaming suds, when Charlie Gregory appeared in the doorway.

"You?" Becca exclaimed. She had imagined their meeting very differently. She had dreamed about it in a dozen variations, and yet Charlie's appearance was so startling, there was a kind of magic in the flesh-and-blood fact of his being there. "Oh, Charlie, is it really you?"

"Take a look," he replied, laughing. "All you have to do is touch me; see for yourself. How about a kiss, just so you'll be sure?"

"Not like this, Charlie. I'm a sight to behold." For the first time Becca was aware of her appearance.

"I'll not be denied," Charlie insisted. "I demand a credit voucher."

"We'll see," Becca said, drying her arms and feeling suddenly shy.

"Am I very different?" Charlie asked her.

They scrutinized each other cannily, looking for changes. He was clearly a young man who had been separated from home and its comforts. In veterans' talk, Charlie had seen the elephant, which meant poor food, little sleep, exhaustion, and yes, Becca felt it, he had known fear beyond her understanding, mastered it, and grown in consequence. Yet for all that, it was Charlie safe, and so she insisted, "You haven't changed a bit," until her basic honesty forced Becca to relent. "How spent you look, Charlie. Your eyes . . ."

"Long train ride," he passed it off, yet less-recent experiences had etched a line of bewilderment between his eyes, "and not a mark that won't come off in a hot tub."

"I don't suppose you're discharged," she asked cautiously.

"In a way," he replied. "Officially, I'm on detached recruiting service. After that it's up to me to decide."

That night Becca wrote in her journal, "Charlie Gregory caught me with my sleeves rolled up and my hair down in the kitchen, looking like old Harry. I must have frightened him though he invited me to go for a ride tomorrow. We'll be picking up Alex."

It was the morning of Christmas Eve when the three friends got together. "Just like old times," Alex said contentedly. "Not a thing seems to have changed."

"What's the same?" Becca said. "You've got a limp, and we're all lots older now and more serious."

"Are we?" Charlie asked sadly.

What they had all discovered, without putting it into words, was a sense of mortality.

"Jonesville's the same," Alex said, "and still in a way I do feel old, and yet newborn somehow."

When a train passed heading west, only Charlie stood up in the buggy and waved. No passenger waved back. The windows were shut against the cold, but the three friends glanced at each other. It was like looking into a mirror for a split second and recognizing oneself. They all laughed.

"Westward ho," Alex said.

"No fancy women this time. Wounded, or prisoners maybe," Charlie speculated. "Or workers. The Union Pacific's begun laying tracks. Soon you'll be able to ride all the way to San Francisco on the cars, but what's the fun in that?"

With the train gone and the buggy sitting still on the hillside, they could hear the wind in the bare branches, a melancholy sound. The sun by now lay on the western horizon, and its slanting rays felt as cold as the moon's. "Smells like snow," Becca said, smiling. Inside her head she heard the merry jingling of sleigh bells.

"How about practicing Christmas carols?" Alex asked, and with the buggy homeward bound they sang one after another all the way. How long had it been since Becca had sung out loud? Ages.

Christmas Eve meant holly and ivy on the mantel, green ivy, red holly berries around the portrait of old Grandma Cronk in the hall, holly and ivy for the soldier boys come home safe. Becca's father popped corn and she made candy, admitting in her diary that it was slightly burned. Becca helped her mother make doll clothes for the girls next door, and finally they decorated the tree. While the tree stood, Becca knew she would be safe. Somehow the tree brought into the Case house forces that were good and sheltering. Last of all, they hung their stockings. "Will Santa bring me something on the morrow?" she speculated in her diary. Only with the lamp extinguished did Becca notice that it had begun to snow.

All night snow fell outside the shuttered window, and by morning Jonesville was another North Pole. Its houses wore caps and eyebrows of thick white, and when the boys came to visit they used the Forman sleigh. Becca's mother offered them Christmas pudding, to which her father surreptitiously added a generous dollop of rum. It was only once a year. Then there were carols and because Charlie was silent, Becca heard her mother reprimanding him in song, "You're not singing, you're not singing . . . Alleluia . . . You're not singing." To which Charlie responded, "Honestly, Mrs. Case, I was just remembering how my father once said I couldn't carry a tune in a chamberpot."

"Charles Gregory, what a thing to say," she admonished him, "and besides, I happen to know you're a very fine singer." Then Becca's father smoothed it over with, "Blame it on the rum, Mrs. Case," but Charlie was obliged to take the lead in "The Twelve Days of Christmas," after which Becca's mother said, "There, didn't I tell you so?" Really, they were all far too happy to worry about anything.

Before the boys headed home, there were presents. From her parents Becca received her heart's desire, a red silk dress, while Alex presented her with a leather-bound book of old New York, as well as what he described as a special present and not for Christmas at all. This was a morocco album tooled in gold and signed on the first page, "Alex A. Forman, U.S. Army."

"I love it," she told him, "but I wish you hadn't put that U.S. Army."

Becca offered her final attempt at socks to both boys, and Charlie presented her with earrings. Becca turned away to hide her pleasure while Charlie admitted they were only gilt on brass. One day, he promised, they would be gold. "That's a solemn pledge, Bec," and she beamed back at him, shone back at him. Catching herself finally, she turned to Alex, saying, "What a thoughtful gift. I'll begin reading the book tonight, and you must write something in the album, both of you."

Last of all, they lit the tiny candles on the tree. These burned with a fine and consuming brilliance, yet even as Becca delighted in their glow, they began to sputter and fade.

During the holidays, time lost meaning for Becca. One day ran into another until at midnight on New Year's Eve cannon were fired in the square. With such an exclamation point, 1862 ended and 1863 began. "I hope it's a better year for us all," she whispered in what was close to being a prayer. On January 1 they all attended the annual holiday ball, about which Becca wrote in her journal, "There was over eighty couples besides crowds of lookers on. There was scant room to dance but I enjoyed it well under the circumstances." That was how the holiday passed, and the next day her father took down the tree because he always did, even though Becca asked him to wait a few days, and with this, her sense of security began to evaporate.

# ELEVEN

*Springtime for Fighting Joe*

THE REAL WORLD RETURNED with the *Jonesville Weekly Independent*'s announcement that the emancipation of slaves was now official. "If we can only make Johnny Reb toe the line," Becca's father said. "No one seems to think old Burnside's the man for the job."

Alex had received a letter from his half brother, William McCarthy, who served with General Grant on the Mississippi.

Bill wrote:

> Grant is a good man, not a drinker like some say, and given the time and the men, I think he might win this war. As for myself I have had a very bad cold for several days which kept me somewhat unwell on account of my lungs but I am getting better and I think I'll be in good health when the weather warms.

"I worry about him some," Alex admitted.

"Grant?" Franklin Case asked.

"No, my brother Bill. He's never been robust. I'm the one who ought to represent my family in this war, not Bill."

The war again. Becca felt it was unlucky to speak of it, and her spirits lifted when a snowstorm spread out of the west. They all seemed to brighten at the first sight of the low, tumbling rollers and the rising wind that sang in the trees. "You can smell a big storm before it arrives," her father said as he set about latching the shutters. Soon infinite flakes fell on Jonesville, shining like iron filings in the yellowing lights, falling in swift screens, making footprints vanish as they were printed. Perhaps it would never stop—then the boys must forget about patriotic duty and going back to war. With this thought Becca slept soundly in the rushing blackness. By morning the snow had slackened, though the sky remained dark with promise.

Storm after storm washed over Michigan that winter. Time passed slowly, and Becca saw less of Alex and Charlie than she liked, but it was enough knowing they were safe. They visited when they could, beating off the snow before the stove. Becca felt it was like a winter in the old days: popping corn, sleighing through town, even an oyster party, with Charlie and Alex boiling them up into a fine New England stew, just perfect with the wind whistling in the eaves.

The only bad thing was news from Pulaski that Julia was having a difficult pregnancy. Becca and her mother took the cutter, pulled by two horses, and got through. Both concluded that, with Julia, complaints exceeded afflictions, and on January 25 Becca recorded, "When a man marries, his troubles begin, is the old saying, and it seems to be the case with my brothers."

For a while even the trains were not getting through, nor was the news. Jonesville was late in hearing of Burnside's mid-January mud march, a failed attempt to outflank Lee again, which led to the general's dismissal.

"And none too soon," Charlie said. Joseph Hooker was

Burnside's replacement. Fighting Joe, the soldiers called him. "Can't be any worse," Charlie added unenthusiastically, while Hooker was quoted in the paper boasting of crossing the Rappahannock and seizing the enemy. He still had one hundred twenty thousand men to do the job.

There were no more winter storms in Jonesville, though for a long time the cold silence of the snow held sway. Becca wrote in her diary, "Last Monday was my birthday, and I forgot to notice it in any manner. Just think how fast I'm growing old. Time has seemed so short since I was a little schoolgirl of ten. Hope I shall grow wiser and better as time leaves its tracks."

Then one day there was a faint sort of music, water flowing. Charlie came by, leaving muddy footprints. "Feels like spring," he said. "Kind of day I get the old itch."

"For what?" Becca asked, fearing he meant the army.

"You know, the open road. Pa keeps telling me it's something I'll outgrow, but now with the public lands opening up out West, a hundred and sixty acres for the taking. . . ." he mused. "You know, I had a dream about you last night."

"Oh?" She looked away, giving herself time to blush. "What did you dream?"

"Just the old going west thing again. I used to think that by running fast I could leave it all behind."

"And can't you?"

"Now I sort of think running only completes the circle sooner."

Becca was ready to speak. She felt herself skimming the edge of a verbal abyss. Her upper lip lifted slightly. It proved to be only a conversation with herself. She looked at her hands.

"A penny for your thoughts, Bec."

"Oh, nothing, just thinking."

"You look so pretty when you're thinking, I can't help myself," and he kissed her until Becca twisted her face away with a little gasp. "Sorry. I didn't mean to be rude, but you're so beautiful today. And, well, it's sort of a good-bye kiss."

"What do you mean, good-bye?" she asked, full of suspicion and a sudden chill.

"Becca, you can call me a fool and a liar, but I've reenlisted."

"Reenlisted! I could have predicted it." She was furious. "But why? After all this time, why now?"

"And why do women always expect you to be in the same place where you were last?"

"I asked you first, Charlie Gregory. Why?"

"Well, I suppose it's because of the proclamation." She was confused. "Emancipation. You might say I have a cause now." She was startled by the gathering ice in his gray eyes. "I mean, if we win, we change the world. We must change the world, Bec, or have no victory. You can see that."

"I appreciate your telling me," Becca replied coldly. "I think I just may go to New York. I haven't seen my sisters there in years. With you leaving, and Alex talking about taking a job up in Wisconsin or maybe limping off as a soldier again, well, why shouldn't I?" she asked defiantly.

Alex's decision was slower in coming, though perhaps it was an inevitable response to events. With the help of God, surely the Union must win, but with the spring, they seemed to be losing still. General Hooker had put the Army of the Potomac back on its feet, straightened up the sloppy camps, limited desertions, seen that the men were again paid and well fed, well drilled, and given furloughs home. "My plans are perfect," said General Hooker. "May God have mercy on General Lee, for I will have none."

Then on April 13 he began his move, yet another attempt

to outflank Lee. Spirits were high in the balmy Virginia spring-time. Anemones and violets flowered beside the roads. Cherries and apples blossomed while the bands played "The Girl I Left Behind Me." By April 30 the Union army was crowding into Chancellorsville, where they first met opposition, Confederate cavalry led, as usual, by Jeb Stuart.

Panicked deer bursting from the thickets of the wilderness were Hooker's first clue that Stonewall Jackson had marched his men around the Union flank. The wild, weird rebel yell came at dusk, and shaken by a near miss, Hooker later admitted, "To tell the truth, I just lost confidence in Joe Hooker." It was another rout, with small consolation to be derived from the news that Lee's favorite, General Jackson, had been accidentally wounded in the dark by his own men.

Bad news came also from the Ward-Master, General Hospital Number 3, in Nashville, Tennessee. Dated May 4, 1863, and addressed to Alex, it read:

Sir,

This evening it becomes my duty to inform you, as a friend and soldier of the death of Wm. H. McCarthy of Co. G, 18th Michigan, who died in this hospital today of typhoid pneumonia. He was well dressed in his uniform and will be well buried tomorrow. His effects are with me and in my charge and will remain with me until someone of his near friends or his administrator sends for them.

Alex's reaction to the news seemed to exceed the somewhat distant relationship he had always had with his older half brother, but he was worried about his mother's reaction. She had heard the news of William's death while recovering from a heavy cold, and the shock had sent her to her bed. Her cough, always present, had become much worse.

Becca and Charlie were talking about Alex when he found them in the Case parlor. They both looked up, startled by his silent appearance. Becca seemed to sigh, and Alex felt he had intruded upon a tryst.

"Don't frown so, Alex," Becca admonished him. "It makes you look so old and severe."

Alex was momentarily bewildered, and the freshness of her smile moved him to forget what he meant to say, though the scene only served to harden his resolve, which he revealed to Becca later when he found her alone. "I've decided to return to the Seventh," he said.

"Not you, too! Oh, Alex, I thought you had better sense."

He tried to explain his reasons to her. Now, with William gone, he was the only one left to represent his family in a cause that he believed, heart and soul, to be just. "Besides," he added, "you're in love with Charlie. I've seen how you look at him."

"Don't, Alex."

"Well, he's my best friend. I'm glad it's him, and I guess I know how to lose."

"Alex, you're saying that, not me. You know how fond I am of you."

"Very fond," he repeated, wanting blind devotion.

"If only you could be a little less reasonable," she said, making it sound like a fault, "a little more, well, insane."

"Like Charlie?" he asked her sadly. It always seemed to come back to that.

"Oh," she said with exasperation, "I didn't say that, either. You and Charlie both . . . I don't know." She stepped to the window, not knowing what to say.

Disgusted with men, Becca wrote East that night, accepting her two married sisters' long-standing invitations. Then she went to the window and looked out into the dark night. "If I cry," she told herself, "my cheek may freeze right here to the glass."

There was no fanfare when it came time for Alex and Charlie to depart. Both boys had paid their respects together the previous evening. "I scarcely know how to say good-bye to either of you," Becca admitted.

"Then don't." Alex kissed her discreetly, but fondly, on both cheeks, but Charlie, always unpredictable, buried his face in her hair. Becca would never forget how he looked that evening, bursting with health, a young man who had come close to knowing what he must and wanted to do.

"Will you come to the train?" Alex asked. It would be departing from the Jonesville depot at about six in the morning.

"If it were up to me, you wouldn't be going then or any other time."

"Then this is good-bye," he concluded. Alex was not one to insist or argue.

"Yes, good-bye."

"Is it necessary to be so to the point?" Charlie asked. He still held her hands. "I have this feeling I may never—"

"Everyone feels that way," Alex interposed.

"Nothing will happen to you, Charlie. To either of you." Becca spoke firmly, but there was an imploring note in her voice, for she sensed long, lonely journeys and great hazards.

"No, nothing will happen to us," Alex said. "I promise you that, as long as we look out for each other."

"Charlie, you're hurting my hands." There was a pause until he raised her hands and kissed them both before she could withdraw. Becca gave him an uncertain glance, then pulled her hands gently away.

"And you take care, too," Alex admonished. "New York's a big city. There are dangers there, too."

When they had left to go to their homes and pack, Becca felt badly. She scarcely slept, and rose before dawn, determined to walk to the depot. From the front porch she heard the whuff-whuff of tired steam. A few passengers were climbing into the cars, which were soon in accelerating motion. Becca's throat choked up; her eyes stung with tears. Faster and faster the train pulled away. It was over, ended; yet, they'd promised to write. It wasn't that far to the Potomac, but Becca knew in her heart it would be a long time and that more than time and distance would stand between them.

Becca began her own packing for New York that night. It was June of 1863, and despite herself, these preparations lifted her spirits. She took scarce note of her father's commentary on the newspaper. "It says here, General Lee's moving his army north again."

"And what's that supposed to mean, Pa?" To which his hands rose and fell, a limp gesture of uncertainty. Who could say?

# TWELVE

## Gettysburg: "Seventh Michigan Rally Here"

CHARLIE AND ALEX ARRIVED BACK with their regiment, which was posted along the Potomac west of the capital city, in time to benefit from the issue of new Springfield rifles. The new guns were lighter than the battered Enfields to which they had become resigned. General Hooker had just been dismissed and self-effacing General Meade put in command. "That damned goggle-eyed old snapping turtle," some called him. In the southwest, after a small victory at Champion's Hill, General Grant had settled down before Vicksburg, Mississippi, on what seemed like a permanent basis; rumor had it that Grant was drinking again. Otherwise, little had changed.

"Same old regiment," Alex said, wondering if there'd been any sense to his reenlisting.

"Same old mess," Charlie agreed. They were both tired from the trip and, as it turned out, had only a few days to recuperate. On June 27 their regiment was detailed as wagon guard. After breakfast they marched northwest for Urbana, Maryland, arriving there at three o'clock the following morning after a hike of thirty-seven miles. Only the presence of the wagons, on which Alex had ridden most of the way, with an increasing number of others, kept him going.

Next morning the Seventh Michigan set off smartly, in columns of four, down the rutted road, baked hard by the sun. It was still the cool of the morning, and now Maryland lay behind them. Marching developed a rhythm of its own, the steady drumming of feet, the clang of metal on metal, conversations that died as the heat and the dust rose. By midmorning they were creatures of the dust, inhaling the poison silently, wondering who would fall out first. They showed no martial spirit now, but coughed and spat cottony saliva onto the valley road. At the Monocacy River, their new commander, Colonel Amos Steele, called a judicious halt. The afternoon was taken off entirely, in anticipation of the long march to Uniontown, Pennsylvania, the following day: thirty-two miles to be covered in twelve hours. Again Alex rode the last few hours, with his and Charlie's rifles beside him. "A few more days like this, heading northwest, and we'll be home in Michigan." That was the joke going around, but there wasn't much laughter.

As they approached Uniontown, all who rode were shamed into taking to their feet with their arms shouldered, since the townsfolk had seen no armies before and waited to cheer. The colors were broken out as they formed up again into columns of four. Then the band struck up "John Brown's Body," or "The Battle Hymn of the Republic," as a few were beginning to call it. Little boys trotted along beside the plodding men, doing cartwheels in their excitement, pretty girls in white dresses leaned on white picket fences and waved, while the soldiers tried to smile back at them from dry, cracked lips. Alex counted each painful step, willing himself not to fall. For many who watched and wondered and cheered them, this was the only road they had ever traversed. For the boys and men plodding by, most of them veterans now, this was simply one more endless dusty road, but for many it was the last they would ever know.

Just beyond town a field had been set aside, and the exhausted Seventh Michigan emptied into it. "Alex, don't let things get you down," Charlie said, his voice soft and husky, with all his weariness rising to the surface in a great, indrawn sigh.

"I just hate for the old Seventh to look like that, marching through a cheering crowd."

"Well, we made it," Charlie said as he sat down heavily on the trampled ground. "That's the main thing." Maybe it was, but if they were chasing Lee's army, and if they caught up, how could they possibly fight as well? Alex wondered. Their cause was just. He believed in it heart and soul, as did Charlie, yet they were losing and, it seemed, must lose again here in western Pennsylvania, or New Jersey, or Washington, or wherever Lee chose to turn upon them. For weren't their generals always failures, while the Confederates could say, "I've heard of God, but I've seen General Lee."

No rations were distributed that night. They had only the hardtack that they had carried and water from a nearby stream to fill their canteens. Charlie sat propped against a tree, shoes and stockings off, the soles of his feet like open sores, and wrote to Becca:

Dear Bec,

Does it sound like an insult to say you're a soldier's girl?

There was a smile on his face as he tapped the stub of his pencil against his chin.

He's in Jonesville, Alex realized. I wish I could be. But Alex could not lift his thoughts from the field of exhausted men or the battle they faced, tomorrow or the day after that. I'm no coward, he told himself, yet he had a dark premonition that he was marked for death as surely as a character in a Shakespeare tragedy, and he wrote to Becca:

Remember, Becca, you can count on Charlie through thick and thin. He's a lot more steady than he lets on.

"Don't look so glum, Alex," Charlie said, pausing in his own writing. "Things'll work out. I don't know why, but I have a feeling."

"Maybe," Alex concurred, "if we stick together."

"We will, so don't worry about it. After all, when does lightning ever strike twice at the same place? I mean, I'm the one who ought to be worried." He gave a short laugh. "Alex, I've something for Bec." He answered Alex's startled look with a reassuring smile. "Just in case . . . You look after it for the next few days, just in case."

Alex had such a foreboding before every battle, needing only to close his eyes to see the glitter of bayonets and muskets aimed at his heart. "Charlie, I can't recall you losing your confidence before."

"Nights, sometimes," Charlie admitted sheepishly.

" 'Thou shalt not be afraid for any terror by night, nor for the arrow that flieth by day,' " Alex quoted.

"Actually, it's the bullets that worry me," Charlie countered, and lay down with his head pillowed on his arms. "But I don't intend losing any sleep over it, mind," and he yawned, so that in sympathy Alex was obliged to yawn back.

"Am I keeping you up?" Alex said after a moment of silence.

"Oh," Charlie started, "not a bit." But it had been a long day, and there was no reason to suppose tomorrow would not be harder still, the supreme test that generals liked to talk about. "Well, on second thought, yes."

"Just remember," Alex said, "we stick together, come what may."

On the last day of June, the Seventh marched again, in sweltering heat and dust. Now farm carts full of children and chickens passed them on the road, and there were rumors of hostile armies gathering. It seemed more than rumor the following morning, when three days' worth of field rations were passed out.

On July 1 the weather was hotter still. The regiment marched all morning, taking to the roadside because of the dust thrown up by the wagons and artillery pieces. At noon the column halted, no telling for how long, and the Seventh, which was reduced by now to fourteen officers and a hundred and fifty men, had barely settled into the inky shade of a grove of apple trees when there arose the neighing of horses, and gallopers appeared on the road.

"I don't like the look of that," Charlie said, and he was right. Presently a bugle stammered, and Colonel Steele sat his horse beside the road. "Double quick, boys," he shouted, "we march to the sound of the guns."

Once over the next rise of ground, they heard the cannonade, a distant grumble still. "Lord, I do wish that was thunder for a change," Alex observed.

By the time they camped four miles southeast of a little town called Gettysburg, the day had cooled and the stillness of evening was in the air. The Seventh Michigan camped on the top of a conical hill. Pickets were posted and fence rails were scavenged from the farm fields and piled into defensive breastworks. Again there were reports of heavy fighting up ahead. Five regiments from the Middle West had been led against the enemy, with fifes shrilling out, "The Campbells Are Coming." As so many times before, the Union forces had been cut up, and General Reynolds was shot from his horse.

"It must have been bad," Charlie commented. "Generals don't plan on being killed."

"But maybe it's over. Maybe we're too late this time." Alex didn't sound disappointed.

"Maybe," Charlie agreed.

Still, there didn't seem any use hanging onto their rations; even salt pork wouldn't last long in the summer heat. They made a fire from twigs and small branches, broiling the tough meat on the tips of their bayonets in a swirl of sparks and insects.

"I used to think food tasted a heap better over an open fire," Charlie mused. "Guess I was just a fool kid, pretending to be a mountain man or something." He turned the darkening lump so that drops of fat fell off and crackled into the embers.

"Smells pretty good," Alex encouraged. The flickering flames embalmed his face. Not wanting to see his supper cook down to a hard crisp, Alex blew on his portion, moving it gingerly from hand to hand. With a, "Guess this'll have to do," he popped the blackened pork into his mouth. "Ma never would have punished me with this stuff," he reflected, and with eyes closed, he chewed resignedly, with near fatalistic determination. Except for the methodical motion of his jaws he might have been asleep. He nearly was.

It was a short night. Reveille sounded before three A.M. The camp was struck. Other buglers repeated the call up and down the road that led on into Gettysburg. There was only the calling of crows when the Seventh Michigan broke camp and moved into column at five o'clock the morning of that second day of July 1863. The first signs of a battle were the field hospitals, set out with yellow flags that drooped in the dawn hush. The town of Gettysburg, small even by Jonesville standards, appeared off to the right as they trudged up the slope of Evergreen Cemetery toward an arched gatehouse and a stern sign that admonished: ALL PERSONS FOUND USING FIREARMS IN THESE GROUNDS WILL BE PROSECUTED WITH THE UTMOST RIGOR OF THE LAW.

The Fifty-Ninth New York was already deploying to the front, in support of a battery of field guns. Here the Seventh went into line, the battery on their left flank, a small thick grove of oaks on their right. Skirmishers prowled forward toward the invisible foe, while Colonel Steele directed the others to erect rail barricades, behind which Alex and Charlie lay down as the sun and the heat rose together.

"I suppose they're out there," Alex said. He assumed the Confederates would attack as soon as the sun was fairly up, but that did not shock him. He was too punch-drunk with effort and lack of sleep to be shocked by anything.

"They always are," Charlie replied, wondering why the Army of the Potomac was inevitably greater, except where the fighting took place. Well, it looked like a long line spreading left and right, judging from glimpses of activity he had on the edge of the trees there. Still, with any luck, the attack would fall somewhere else. Jackson had a way of surprising them from the rear, but of course he had to remember that Jackson wasn't there anymore.

Skirmishing went on all day—nothing much, like boys out on the Fourth of July with squibs—until a little after four, when the July heat seemed at its most intense. Suddenly the Confederate artillery roared out, and the squat brass smooth-bores to their left replied, leaping at each discharge and tearing the ground as the gunners cheered and cursed and their horses shrilled in terror or pain.

Then the gray ranks came on, with the raging sunlight of

early evening behind them, a gray snake spiked with flapping flags, and the men of the Seventh Michigan crouched low behind their fence rails for those terrible minutes of holding fire, until, with a deep and furious chant, they rose. A sheet of flame and boiling smoke exploded up and down the line. Some of the gunners had already fled. The battery was overrun, but the Seventh was a veteran regiment now. "You won't take this fence!" Charlie yelled at the Confederates, and they did not, but fell back grudgingly, leaving their wounded and dead, along with three stands of colors.

Then Colonel Steele walked the line. "Well done," he kept repeating. "Well done, indeed. Men, I'm proud of you." It was Steele's first fight in command, but the rank and file of the ever-shrinking Jonesville Light Guard was down to a hundred and thirty-one, with ten men wounded and nine more dead on the field, a high percentage of fatalities. Such was the price of fighting from the partial cover of a barricade.

That was all for the second day of July. At nine that evening a band played "Tattoo." Taps sounded presently from afar. No food was to be had. Alex and Charlie shared a pocketful of hardtack, and amid the trunks of oak trees, with their leaves from autumns past still strewn on the earth, they rested, their loaded rifles at their sides, as the summer night came down.

A hazy moon winked at them through the foliage. With a tombstone for shelter, Charlie curled on his side. Sleeping among the dead, and not a care in the world, Alex thought enviously. Beneath a volley of shooting stars the earth lay quiet, save for a farmer's dog who could not accept so many strangers in his field. It sounds like Jonesville, Alex thought. I might be home. There was not even the cry of an injured man. The stretcher bearers must have done their work for a change. Eventually, out of sheer weariness and emotional upheaval, Alex also slept, only to open his eyes, after a profound sleep that seemed to last but minutes, to see a pale infusion in the eastern sky announcing another day. Again it was tomorrow.

Alex had to pry open one of Charlie's eyes to waken him. "Come out of there," he said. "It's time to rise and shine."

"I'll rise," Charlie said, "but I don't expect to shine. Where are we?" He sounded genuinely confused. Alex had to remind him, adding, "And where were you?"

"Out West," Charlie said, stretching. "When I'm asleep, I become what I dream."

"Was I there?" Alex asked.

"You?" Charlie burst into boyish laughter. It had saved him in many tight situations.

"Becca was, I'll bet."

"I'll keep my dreams to myself, thank you," Charlie replied, smiling as if he knew something about Alex that Alex did not know about himself. "Don't look so hurt," and he punched Alex affectionately on the shoulder. He sat up and looked around. "I don't suppose Johnny Reb's gone on home? No."

There was nothing to eat. With half a canteen of water between them, little remained beyond awaiting developments. Charlie leaned wearily on his rifle, as though upon the handle of a plow. The sky was a deep, bottomless blue well, pulsing with heat. "It's bound to rain before long," he said. When artillery opened on the distant flanks he remarked, "No, they haven't skedaddled after all." When the cannonade broke off at ten o'clock, "Now maybe they have."

With the renewed silence, Colonel Steele again walked before his men, repeating his message to each squad. "Men, you are about to engage in battle. You have never disgraced the state of Michigan. I know you won't on this occasion. If any man runs, I have instructed the file closers to shoot him, and if they fail to do so, I shall myself. That's all I have to say," and on down the line he walked.

"I'm not sure I cotton to this Colonel Steele," Charlie said.

"He could show more respect," Alex concurred.

"He could at least get some food up this way." But a creaking water wagon was all that made the rounds.

Heat rose, simmering through midday, and at exactly 1:07 P.M. a signal gun off to the right delivered its thudding report. Immediately lightning flickered the length of the Confederate line, flashing in and out among the trees. Presently Union guns replied, and the shrieking, moaning, whistling cacophony blended into a strange absence of sound that seemed to absorb lesser noises. To communicate, Alex and Charlie had to cup their hands to each other's ears. "Remember, we stick together!" Alex shouted. They shook hands on this. It was a vow they'd made to Becca. Then they lay down behind the fence rails while the missiles screamed overhead.

A shout went down the line as General Winfield Hancock rode by on his rearing horse. For nearly three hours the smoke and fire of the artillery duel kept up. Then slowly the Federal guns fell silent. Presently the enemy guns did the same, and a strange quiet returned, a numb, dumb admission to them all. Alex's teeth had gone funny. Had he tried to drink from a glass, they would have bitten right through. Charlie kept yawning, great, jaw-aching, carnivorous yawns. "What next?" he asked.

"Go buy a cheap coffin," Alex replied, knowing that presently they'd be fixing bayonets. All hardened veterans now, neither side was made for easy defeat. They might be destroyed by artillery down to the last man, but never defeated, and all the faces of the men up and down the line, like so many waxwork dummies, had calm, determined expressions, extraordinarily tense and self-possessed, yet pale as the death that hovered over them.

Presently the Confederate brigades streamed out of the thick woods that had hidden them. Far across the rolling wheat fields, they formed into lines with what seemed parade-ground care. All Alex and Charlie could do was watch, as they might any spectacle. Finally the first skirmishers moved out. They did not look like much, simply brown-and-gray dots. Even when they began to shoot, it had no meaning after the cannonade. Then the long lines moved forward with their banners, as slowly as though on parade, exactly as Alex had imagined the scene the day before in a fit of depression. Those lines spread away on either side. How many young men trod the ripe wheat down, their flags lifting and sagging with the rolling ground, yet slowly growing, as in a dream?

Bayonets rasped into sockets up and down the Michigan line. No firing yet. Then the artillery opened up again through the clearing smoke. Lord, Alex thought, almost a prayer, please stop them before they get here. But what would God be doing in such a hellish place as this? He had never seen so many men committed to one fight.

The Confederates surged into a valley, came out again, moving faster. Colonel Steele began shouting, "Hold your fire, boys, hold your fire!" until through the shredded smoke came those lunging strangers Alex had seen at Fair Oaks, sounding that familiar, shrill, earsplitting cry. By now the battery on their left was firing canister, ripping red gaps in the advancing line, and the Seventh was engaged, too, each man firing, sheltering, reloading; firing as fast as he could, tearing paper cartridges with his teeth as his mouth turned black, cursing his rifle, cursing the rebs, clanging home his ramrod, one more round to turn them back before their bayonets stabbed through the smoke. Minié balls whined and meowed overhead. Veterans in their old age would tell their grandchildren how the rebs must have run out of ammunition and begun hurling kittens instead.

Alex was at first unaware that the Southern charge was angling away toward the left-hand battery, a gray colonel out front with his black hat thrust forward on the tip of his sword. He did see his own Colonel Steele running along in front of the barricade, gesticulating and shouting in a cracked voice for them to follow him. A bugle chattered somewhere nearby, and Alex became part of a surging crowd.

"Guide on the colors, double time!" It seemed to be the colonel's voice still.

"Charlie?" Alex was over the barricade before he remembered his friend. "Let's go, Charlie!" There was no turning back. The rebs had piled into the battery. Now the colonel was calling on them to pile into the rebs.

A sense of unreality seized Alex. He felt as he might in a dream, striding without ever touching the ground, fatally resigned, almost drowsy as he withdrew into a secret hiding place deep within himself that was warm and secure, while on the outside his hands felt burnt from the gun he kept firing. He crashed unheeding through bruising thickets, saw darting figures in butternut, fired on them in the smoke, caught his foot on the trail of an overturned gun, sprawled there face-down, remembering, amid the wildcat screeching, a girl named Becca.

As Alex rose painfully, the red and blue of flags broke from the roiling clouds of smoke. A horse loomed before him, its head thrown back over an arched neck. Hooves slashed down like the blur of wings, striking at his face. With a whistling cry, the horse lunged backward with a half-dozen pounding strides, like a great mechanical toy. Alex rolled away, fired again, ran forward with the others, called Charlie's name, and then suddenly he was down on his back, with a taste of powder in his mouth.

Alex felt no pain, only surprise, but he knew what it was like to be hit. At first he did not know where, and then his hand found the place: the left thigh again. Fresh blood oozed, unbelievably, from the same old wound. As Alex pressed his hand to his leg, he felt a kind of giddy mirth and said out loud, "Charlie, what did you say about lightning?" and when there was no immediate response, "Charlie, where are you?" All around him fighting still raged. For a moment Alex thought he heard Charlie calling his name, but how could that be? Charlie was sensibly out west, way out west with Becca. I want to be there too, Alex thought. Wait for me, Charlie. And then the darkness closed about him.

When Alex regained consciousness, he realized someone lay beside him, breathing hard and gazing at the sky. "Charlie?" he said, but it wasn't his old friend. "You look as tattered as I feel, reb," he muttered, and the answer came back weakly, "We-uns don't dress up in our Sunday best to butcher hogs."

"We're both of us damaged goods, for sure," Alex replied. He felt no animosity now.

"I'm parched," the other admitted.

There was water in Alex's canteen, and he tried to pull himself, on his elbows, to the fallen foe, who bent and straightened his legs as though working a treadmill, repeating all the while, "Our Father who art in heaven." With a last effort, Alex got the canteen to the man's lips, held it there until it was nearly empty, then collapsed.

Alex woke to feel a cool film on his face, dew or the trace of a passing shower. He lay still, staring at the misty moon, remembered the staggering flags and the smoke pierced with lightning. The rebel soldier still lay beside him. "There's a tad more water, friend," Alex whispered, though his own thirst was terrible now. "Another few drops?" But the reb did not move, and Alex began to realize that all those around him were dead. For a time he forced himself to stay awake, lest death take him by surprise.

Again Alex slept, awakening to see horsemen silhouetted against the dawn. The sun rode on their shoulders. Weakly Alex called out to them, "Look here, I'm alive. I'm still alive." But the men rode on, unhearing, and Alexander Aberdeen Forman was left among the dead upon the field. Of the Jonesville Light Guard, twenty-one had been killed, among them Colonel Amos E. Steele. Charles W. Gregory was reported missing in action.

# THIRTEEN

# *New York Burning*

EIGHT YEARS HAD PASSED since Becca had lived in Brooklyn, time enough for the world to turn itself upside down, yet she felt instantly at home in this room with its canopied bed, for the bed had once stood in her parents' house in this city. Still, between her sister's Brooklyn house and her own home now in Jonesville stretched all those miles. There had been a delay in her departure in order to find a suitable older lady who might be going to New York and could chaperone Becca's journey.

The adventure had finally begun two weeks earlier, when her father had carried Becca's luggage to the depot, a consideration prompted in part by her farewell horseback ride, a wild one, even by Becca's reckoning, that had ended in a fall. Limping painfully and cane in hand, she had boarded the cars in Jonesville with Mrs. Shattuck, a neighbor's aunt. The two women had changed trains at Toledo and then again, at four in the morning, at Cleveland. They changed yet again at Dunkirk, New York, and finally boarded the New York and Erie Railroad to Jersey City, where they had taken the ferry to New York City. At the Manhattan ferry landing, Mrs. Shattuck had been met by her son and Becca by her sister Sarah and Sarah's husband, Tunis Bergen. Sarah, a new bride when Becca last saw her, was now the mother of two girls.

Sarah had run through the crowd at the ferry slip and hugged Becca. "Rebecca Frazer Case, you've grown up!"

"I should hope so," Becca had replied, clinging to her sister. She still despaired of her slim figure and would never achieve her goal of being statuesque.

"My, you must be tired from all that traveling." Tunis was negotiating to have her trunk and carpetbag loaded onto the hackney that would take them to the Brooklyn ferry.

"Me, tired?" She wasn't used to speculating on the luxury of being tired, seldom ever was in truth, and at this moment felt buoyed up by exhilaration and a sense of liberation, as though she stood at the bowsprit of a great ship driving into the wind. Homesick? Not likely. This was home, where she had spent the first twelve years of her life, while she had spent the next eight missing the city.

Sarah wanted all the news. Their father was negotiating to trade off the Clarendon House, of which Becca had reluctantly grown fond, for the Haynes Tavern at Pulaski. Becca was sick of moving, and even the prospect of being nearer to Douglas and Julia was not enough. "If I ever marry," she had written in her journal before leaving Jonesville, "I hope it will be to a man neither shiftless nor fickle. I had best stay here for good, for I cannot imagine making that lonely place my home."

She quickly settled in at Sarah and Tunis's home on Seventeenth Street and made her first acquaintance with their two pretty young daughters. The hurly-burly of Brooklyn and New York enraptured her, from Fulton's fish market, with its baskets of gleaming flounder, tubs of shining eels, and heaps of yellow and green crabs, to the wonders of Barnum's Museum, with its endless curiosities from around the world. Already she and Sarah had been to see an educational show there, *Pomp of Cudjo's Cave*, a piece about slavery and escape from rebel bondage. Barnum's also had the wonders of Fiji cannibals and, though she'd seen them in Jonesville, Tom Thumb and his wife, Lavinia. She and Sarah and Tunis had tickets to see Edwin Forrest as King Lear at Niblo's Garden, and she hoped the riots in New York would not prevent them from going.

Tunis had taken half a day off from his work as an insurance adjuster to show her the fairyland of the new Central Park, and they had arrived in late afternoon in time to see the carriage parade of New York's upper crust. Becca had never seen so many beautiful horses or so many fancy dresses and bonnets. If she was still welcome among her relatives come winter, and she hoped she was, she could show her sister her skill at ice-skating on the lake in Central Park, which was illuminated at night by calcium flares. Already she'd enjoyed fireworks on the Fourth of July at City Hall, a display depicting the fight between the *Monitor* and the *Merrimack*.

Becca sat in her room in the house on Seventeenth Street and decided she loved the city best as it was now, at dusk, with its infinite lights coming on, everything old and tawdry put away. In Michigan, when night fell there was darkness absolute. Not here. It was no brave attempt to mask homesickness but unashamed delight that made her eager to sample all the two cities of Brooklyn and New York had to offer.

But now, with the draft riots going on across the East River in New York, Tunis was talking about Becca moving to her other sister's home on Long Island. Her sister Emma and her husband, Carll Burr, lived far out in Commack, in Suffolk County. It was farm country, but different from Michigan. Becca only vaguely remembered her brother-in-law Carll, who was a horseman like Pa, with just as good a sense of humor and easier going than her father. Letters from Emma and Carll tempted her with promises of seaside picnics and a trip to the freethinking village of Modern Times, where the folks were a little crazy and did as they pleased. Becca was intrigued by tales of all the strawberries you could pick for two dollars, but skeptical that the folks of Modern Times walked around naked, if naked was their fancy.

Yet she had to admit some strange part of her would miss the fearful excitement of the draft riots across the river. Two years ago, when the war was new and exciting and meant flags and drums and the boys in blue marching smartly to the depot, Becca could not have understood young men refusing to serve their country. Now, with all the killing, she didn't know what to think. Besides, they said it was the Irish, fresh off the boat, who were refusing the draft, because they didn't want to free the slaves who'd turn around and take less for the few jobs that didn't come with a no-Irish-need-apply tag attached.

Of course, no one besides herself would ever read these thoughts—she'd burn her journal first—but in the event her memory of these exciting days faded with time, Becca thought it prudent to record her impressions. It had all started on Saturday, July 11, 1863, with the announcement of the first draft of men to serve in the army. On Monday the riots began in New York, and she had been too alarmed and excited for reflecting with pen and ink. Now it was Thursday, July 16, and the riot was sputtering out. It almost seems too bad, Becca thought, but, quickly banishing the unworthy thought, instead wrote solemnly, "These are indeed strange times we live in."

She reread what she had written a few days earlier. "July 11, Saturday. A thousand or so names were drawn from some kind of wheel." She had seen the draft list in the Sunday paper, along with the first casualty reports from Pennsylvania at someplace called Gettysburg. Then on Monday morning, bright and early, the mob was in the streets, saying no to the draft with torches and flung paving stones. "We didn't sleep a wink Monday night," she had written, "what with the fires breaking out in New York and talk of its starting up in Brooklyn."

"Bound to happen," her brother-in-law Tunis had said. Perhaps because he was in the insurance business, he liked making predictions and seeing them come true, no matter how dark the consequences. But what could people expect when the mayor had pushed to make New York a neutral city when the war first started, because it would be good for business? Now there were Copperheads and all sorts of hooligans, mostly Irish Becca had been told, trying to raise a muss. They were stringing up free blacks all over the city and had burned down the negro orphanage on Forty-third Street and beat up anyone who looked rich enough to avoid the draft. Becca disapproved of the practice of paying for a substitute to serve in the army, and she knew that in New York most of the replacements were Irish immigrants, which meant that the jobs they left might go to freed slaves.

It was all too complicated to understand. Finally, the police had opened fire on the mob, only to be driven back. Even the Invalid Corps of veteran soldiers hadn't been able to stop the riots at first. But now, after three or four days of bloodshed and fire, it looked as though the tide had turned, though not before hundreds of people had been killed. "Hundreds," Becca mused. That didn't really sound like much, against the rumors of casualties that were coming from Gettysburg.

It turned dark outside while Becca sat at the deal table writing in her small, thoughtful handwriting, dipping her pen into the brass inkwell. She had begun her first journal in 1859. This was number five. "Yes, I do judge the fires over there to

131

be subsiding. God be praised"—supposing God had something to do with it. But she did hope that God was behind the rumor that the Seventh Michigan was among those forces sent north to maintain order in New York, in which case, and this was the joyful part, she would be twice blessed, for it would mean reunion with Alex and Charlie. How lucky she was, now of all times. Surely life was a strange gift. Becca was not often sure what to do with it, but just now it seemed sufficient to be alive here in Brooklyn with the boys about to arrive.

Her only dark concern was the recent battle. By all reports, Gettysburg had been a desperate fight, but a victory this time. Since Alex had almost died after Fair Oaks, Becca had begun to realize that a victory was not always good news and that war was more than glory and patriotic speeches. Upon first hearing of the fighting in Pennsylvania, she had felt a chill, as though someone had walked over her grave.

But if her old notions were shattered, she had not adopted new ones, caring only that the Seventh arrived in New York with both boys safe, and she would hazard visiting them no matter what the risk. Of course, Sarah could not possibly approve, and getting her permission was out of the question. She might have asked Tunis to go with her, but, since the rioting, he was far too busy with insurance claims to take the time. To go without asking would be wicked, possibly dangerous, and no lady would consider it. Moving to the dresser, she saw a small pale face in the mirror staring sternly back at her. Dare she go? In reply, the image broke into a smile.

What Becca did encounter was delay, for the next day Sarah made good her threat, and Becca was put on the steamboat for Northport, to spend the hot weather at Commack on Long Island with Emma and Carll Burr. Her time with them passed quickly and very pleasantly, for the Burrs were a charming couple, with two small sons who were hard to resist.

On July 30 Becca recorded the culinary delights of a picnic on the beach. "We had roast clams, cucumbers, sherry punch and the rest of the goodies. I shall become so fat neither Alex nor Charlie will recognize their Becca." After lunch they had all gone "bathing and ducking" in Long Island Sound and "when the rain began we had to finish the ice cream, lemonade and blackberries fast and skidaddle." That evening she was furnished with a cousin, Alfred Burr, as escort to a country dance, whom Becca confided to her diary was possibly a draft dodger. "If only it had been Charlie or Al-ex instead of Al-fred it would have been just right." Evidently, poor Alfred had hopes, for Becca concluded, "I can't help but laugh at the slam of the door which I gave to his face. Too bad to laugh at the boys especially one who likes you."

News that the Seventh Michigan had not yet arrived in New York made her country exile easier to endure. Not until August 21 did confirmation arrive of the regiment's disposition in the city, by which time Becca had long since taken the train from Deer Park station back to Brooklyn.

"Young ladies do not go about the city without a female companion." This rule was too absolute for Becca to question, so one morning she simply overlooked it. She told Sarah she was going no farther than the nearby Brooklyn Sanitary Commission, that group of worthy ladies who were preparing for another fund-raiser for wounded and ailing soldiers. As she left Seventeenth Street, she waved to Sarah while frowning slightly, in keeping with the solemnity of her errand. There was always time to make good on bandages not rolled.

Once around the corner, Becca's walk became hurried, intent, as she headed for the ferry slip. Ashore in New York, she went with less certainty. Though the regiments were variously posted, headquarters was, she understood, at the Battery, so she headed there, a course from which she did not consciously stray until she blundered into the dismal fringes of Five Points, an area composed of scraps and ends, the ghastly tenements vomiting up their innards into muddy alleys. She was close to hailing a horsecar back to the ferry, when she began to find herself amid double-breasted broadcloth and the plunge and dip of bright hoop skirts: Wall Street, with the Battery beyond. If she had half expected to see the Seventh Michigan drawn up there at attention, flags flying, Becca was disappointed, but a series of questions did bring her to general headquarters.

There a lieutenant, feet up on a desk as though he'd just concluded a large dinner and his stomach was full, was idly reading a *Harper's Weekly*. But, in the presence of an attractive young woman, his manner assumed a measure of parade-ground polish before he turned her over to a grizzled, overage captain who apologized for the colonel's absence but promised to do his best with her questions. Yes, the Seventh Michigan was in New York, but according to the most recent roster— he ran his finger down the page painfully, a slow reader— they were bivouacked on Staten Island. "Yes, miss, Staten Island." Conscious of her dismay, he added, "I am sorry. Is there someone in particular? You can trust me with a message, miss." So she gave him the names. "Two is it, miss? Well, I suppose with a young lady as pretty as yourself . . . Let me check for you. Won't take a minute." He kept talking intermittently, half to Becca, half as though to keep his own engine going. "Ah, yes, here we have it. Seventh Michigan." Again his eyes followed the moving finger. "Forman, you say?" A silence. "And the other one, Gregory?"

"Charles W. Gregory, Junior," Becca told him.

"Forman, A. A., and Gregory, C. W. Yes." The captain looked again at the ledger's cover. "Well, we do have us the Seventh Michigan." At last he looked up. His dark eyes, flecked curiously with gold, were Becca's idea of tiger's eyes, and she felt they were trying to impress some veiled significance into hers.

"Have you heard from these boys recently? Since Gettysburg, that is, miss? Either of them?" She had not. "And I assume you're aware that the Army of the Potomac suffered grievously on that occasion. I can only presume, as they are not listed here, that they did their final duty. You must seek solace in pride, miss."

"I'm sorry, I just can't hear what you're saying," Becca replied. "All this noise." But she was not sure whether the buzzing came from the echoing corridors or originated in her own ears. "Miss?" The captain's voice was a hoarse whisper. He was not enjoying himself anymore with a young woman who might be his own daughter.

"Tell me, please." Her own voice was pleading, not her voice but another voice in hers, for Becca sensed that something unalterably terrible had occurred.

"You see, miss, those still on the roll call are listed here, as well as those wounded and expected back on duty. I can only assume, well, that your friends died for their country."

Dead. Both of them? It was like a charge of birdshot, scattering Becca's senses. She stood there, her hands spread against the sides of her face, and if she breathed at all, it would have required a mirror to show it.

"Miss, if you have the time, you could return. The colonel might be in touch with more current information. You know the army, it makes mistakes. Miss, would you care to sit down?" He might have added, "before you fall down."

"Oh, how funny," Becca said. "Oh, my head's spinning

135

around. Soon I shall begin to laugh," and she did laugh, wildly, close to a sob. She groped for her former command of the world. This might have been a dream with the walls closing about her. If she could only touch something hard and unyielding. What she did touch was the captain's chair, with his help. "Better, miss? Can I bring you a sarsaparilla?"

"I'm fine," she informed him. Actually, the world had come to a stop, and she began to live at a slight remove from herself, regarding her own behavior with embarrassed side-glances. "I shouldn't be here at all, you know. I should be at home."

"I'm certain the colonel will be back shortly. You can wait right where you are."

"Not at all. I mustn't trouble you, sir."

Whenever something critical happened to Becca, she would step out and apart from herself, becoming a curious observer. She was fine, she insisted, would trouble them no further. The captain was just as insistent, allowing her to depart only with a Corporal Everett as escort to the Brooklyn ferry. Becca declined. The captain persisted. Embarrassed now, his voice had a cough waiting in it. The corporal appeared, a young man from a Vermont regiment. "I'd admire to escort you, miss. It would be my distinct pleasure." Becca dried her eyes with the back of her hand, like a child.

"Only to the ferry, mind."

Becca had little memory of the trip back. Her escort was no older than herself. On another occasion, she would have asked his name, remembered it too, but she scarcely recalled their parting or the ferry ride. Sarah was in the kitchen when Becca tiptoed in, and she gained her own room unnoticed. There was New York silhouetted in the bright light of the summer afternoon, in no way reflecting the darkness that Becca sensed had fallen upon the world. For all that, she felt quiet and composed, and she waited for her feelings to assume outward form. The supper hour came and went. Her sister accepted her protestation of exhaustion from the heat and having snacked at the Sanitary Commission.

Eventually Becca lay down on the bed, with its plush drapes and the thin net curtain to protect against the insects up from the river, though sleep came hard as tears. Blood drummed in her ears and her skin was hot and dry. Suddenly the war had lost all meaning, with Alex and Charlie dead. They were gone from the army list, gone from the world, gone because Cassius Clay had called for abolition at the muzzle of a smoking gun, gone because Gypsies had turned up a card. In no way could Becca cope with such thoughts, yet she could not dismiss them.

# FOURTEEN

---

# *Presumed Dead*

PRESUMED DEAD. The two words echoed inside Becca's head all night long. Presumed dead, both of them. She could not believe it. Her sister's husband Tunis had promised to find out more, but the draft riots still disrupted the city, and Gettysburg was a remote region, without a direct railroad connection or telegraph lines. News of the battle came in slow contradictory snatches, though all the newspapers were calling it a joyous victory for the Union. There was less joy in victory than Becca had once supposed. A few voices even doubted the victory. True, General Lee had been turned back from the North, but clearly his Army of Northern Virginia survived to fight again. The real success seemed to have been at Vicksburg, on the Mississippi. General Grant's name was in the news again, and of his triumph in the west President Lincoln said, "The father of waters rolls unvexed to the sea."

Becca made nothing of all this. The only decision that was solidified in her mind was the resolve to go home to Michigan. No matter who went missing in action or was shipped back in a pine box, Pa'd go on racing his trotters and dabbling in hotel keeping, but she'd have solace from Ma. With Ma, Becca could be a little girl again, just for a while. And in Jonesville she might be able to find out more about Alex and Charlie. They couldn't both be dead.

The next morning, Becca confronted Sarah and Tunis with her decision. "Surely not so soon," her sister exclaimed. "You've been here such a short while." Tunis would find out about Alex and Charlie in no time, she said. He had military connections.

His "connections" happened to be Uncle Andrew Case, whose business of undertaking had quickly responded to the demand created by all wars. Sarah invited him for tea. "Someone has to get the boys home," he explained, "the unlucky ones." Uncle Andrew, who was privy to the casualty reports, would keep his eyes and ears open, and meanwhile, if Becca cared for distraction, he happened to have an appointment at the Davids Island military hospital. "Be glad to have you along, niece," he told Becca. "Not a bad excursion. Clear the cobwebs out of your head. They say there's nothing like a change of scene to organize your thoughts."

Before Becca could decline, Sarah had accepted for her. "What a good idea." Though Becca's intention to return soon to Michigan was firm, she could not deny their combined insistence and found herself and Uncle Andrew boarding the seven A.M. cars of the New York and Boston Railroad for New Rochelle. A stage from there and a ten-minute ferry ride carried them to the red-brick army buildings on Davids Island.

Once there, her uncle said, "Just make yourself at home; smell the salt air. I won't be a trice." A few arrangements, and they'd be off on the one o'clock paddle-wheel steamer back to New York. "Perhaps supper at Delmonico's? Would you like that? Can't very well say you've been to the big city without tasting Delmonico's." In response Becca only framed a weak smile. "Not too much sun, mind. Your sister'd never forgive me if I brought you home red as a lobster." So he left her on a bench near the small pier, where a solitary sentinel stood at parade rest. This was not a fortress as Becca would have imagined it—no thick bastions or dark muzzles of cannon. It seemed more like a college campus, with its well-windowed red-brick buildings neatly envined with ivy. It would not have surprised her to see scholars inside, bent over their books.

As she strolled to and fro, the first windows she passed were dark, yielding no clues. Then there was a faintly lit room where figures moved half-seen behind green louvered shutters, green on darker green, like creatures deep in the sea. In the next block of buildings, the windows were thrown open to the salty air. Inside, a lamp burned smokily, casting a coppery light, and Becca's pupils widened like a cat's.

It was more what she saw than the conditions under which she saw it that transfixed her. He lay on a table and his flesh not covered by his hospital gown was pale. At first, he seemed to be sleeping. With a harsh thudding of her heart the name Charlie came to Becca's lips. Of course, the man was not Charlie, but as she watched, two surgeons began to do something to his leg just below the knee, causing the man to thrash against his restraints and scream as piercingly as a trapped rabbit.

"Chloroform! For God's sake, get more chloroform!" someone yelled.

It took three men to force the soldier back onto the table. She saw the pad of chloroformed cloth pressed to his nostrils, and he subsided with a shudder. Soon the surgeons went to work with a saw. They might have been pruning a tree. Presently the still-bandaged limb lay on a pile of straw beneath the table, like well-packaged meat. By this time Becca had returned to her bench, hunched over, and hoped that the sentinel would not take it amiss if she were sick.

"You don't look a bit red." Uncle Andrew was back again, having closed a very satisfactory shipping contract, to judge by his expression. "A full eighteen loved ones," he explained, "and a few odd bits." The latter could be tricky, as the surgeons were not always careful about how they matched up arms and legs. "But a young lady doesn't want to hear about such problems, not on such a glorious day." Andrew Case rubbed his hands in anticipation of the steamer excursion back to the city and the meal thereafter. He hadn't eaten at Delmonico's in ever so long.

After a lugubrious parade of pine boxes up the gangplank, and much signing of invoices by Uncle Andrew, the steamship *Thomas P. Way* cast off for New York, taking in the whitecaps from warm Long Island Sound in mouthfuls and spitting them out again. At first Becca clung to the rail, holding her lips still, trying hard to rise above the nausea that boiled inside her. Sickness came in waves as she clung to the rail and her uncle exulted in the view and the sea air. Finally she could put it off no longer, but turned around, showing her pale face, her hands clutched together at her waist to keep them from going to her mouth.

"I believe I'll go inside," she told him through clenched teeth, then did so, ignoring his protests.

In the saloon the air was warmer still, steam-softened and loud with the clangor of machinery. Through an open hatch, Becca glimpsed sweat-shiny crew members gazing up like robins from a nest, and Becca knew that down below were great ovens that at any moment might explode. Behind a door marked Ladies' Cloakroom, in humiliatingly unladylike fashion, she did what could be postponed no longer.

"There," Becca told herself, "that's better," and it was,

141

immediately so. With Davids Island purged from her system, she reemerged, eyes shaded, squinting through the afternoon glare at the narrowing Sound, blue and vibrant with light—more light than water, it seemed.

"That's Whitestone village over there," Uncle Andrew explained as a small ferry crossed their bow. "We're making good time. I do hope you're enjoying yourself, working up an appetite and all that."

"I am indeed, Uncle," she replied.

Green-brown water creamed around the steamer's high bow. The watery surroundings began to calm Becca's agitated soul. Her heart beat steadily, thoughts simplified. "Captain Kidd sailed these waters," Uncle Andrew was saying, "and buried his gold on these beaches somewhere." Now sea gulls wheeled like flakes of spray behind the *Thomas P. Way* as it neared New York. Their cries seemed larger than their bodies.

That night Becca wrote in her diary, "Uncle very much enjoyed Delmonico's. It is truly a fine restaurant. Once the *Thomas P. Way* sailed beyond Whitestone, I enjoyed the ride exceedingly, and it helped to clarify my thinking, which has not changed. Though I do love New York, I am resolved to go home."

Becca's stubbornness did not fail her now, despite Sarah's wheedling and promises from Emma and Carll of September picnics on the Sound. Had doubts been opened in her resolve, the arrival of a letter extinguished the last hesitancy. It was clearly addressed in her father's handwriting to Rebecca F. Case, care of T. Bergen, but she delayed opening it, for once such a thing was done, it could no longer be undone. "Such foolishness," she admonished herself, slitting the envelope.

In reading the letter, Becca could almost smell her father's cigar, sense the expansive bulge of his waistcoat at eye level as she remembered it from childhood, hear the confident crunch of his boots on the path.

If your mother were not unwell I would not have bothered you. And of course as you undoubtedly know, your beau is home, grievously wounded but you are not to worry. The doctor holds out considerable hope that he will recover.

Her beau? Which one? Becca sank back onto her bed, ready to pull the sheet over herself, face to the wall. She forced herself to eat heartily that night, building her strength for the trip and trials ahead. Sleep came hard. She thrashed in a maze of shallow, unrefreshing dreams, awakening from the last one with a scream. Thereafter her thoughts repeated like sand in an hourglass, always the same sand sifting through.

In the morning, Sarah urged her to talk things over, but Becca could not go on talking, talking. Some things could not be talked, and before nightfall, Tunis returned with her train tickets. "This may be a mistake," he cautioned, after which Becca thanked him and gathered her belongings into one modest trunk, a large hatbox, and a manageable carpetbag. She examined her room, checking the dresser and under the bed. She had forgotten nothing.

"I certainly will miss going back to Commack," Becca admitted. "And you, Sarah." The sisters embraced. "I don't know when I'll be back."

"Oh, you'll be back," Sarah said with confidence.

Finally, Tunis took her to the train, a substantial gesture, since it involved taking two ferries and an omnibus, but in final parting he said only, "So long, Becca." It was an odd, offhand expression, which to her seemed to imply, "See you again soon," but Becca knew her life would have to be very different, the world very different, before she returned to New York.

The first leg of Becca's journey this time was north to Albany. There she caught the New York Central to Buffalo and points west. She had never liked trains; the sound of them made her shiver. Clearly a train was an agent of death and separation, and she sat in a rear car for fear that the boiler might explode or they would have a head-on collision.

Once darkness fell, the passengers became numb with thwarted sleep. A lantern near either door illuminated the car with artificial dusk, and beyond the clash of rails, the only sound was the stealthy murmur of abandoned paper. The windows were closed against the soot from the engine, and Becca felt perspiration, almost like dew, envelop her body.

Becca could not sleep. Through the streaked window she saw stars and streamers of smoke torn from the engine like some spectral cavalcade. Presently the train headed downhill, going steadily faster, and she wondered if the engineer were asleep with the throttle open. All night the train thundered along, and Becca sat wide awake, waiting for the wreck.

Toward dawn, as the heat rose, a rebellion of passengers took place. Windows were thrown open, and with the rush of air came soot. Becca yearned for a horse of her own and sparkling meadows. She drank some cold tea from the basket Sarah had prepared, but the bread had gone stale and hard and the apples soft and brown.

A stop at Detroit allowed time to rinse her face and hands. A few other passengers descended to do the same, but most simply waited, stupefied, on the cars, peering out across the platform with bored hope. Human sounds mingled with the woof-woof of spent steam as the black engine sent its cloudy breath high. Finally came a whistle. The train shivered like a big dreaming dog, and with gathering speed they headed west again, west toward the afternoon sun. Had not Charlie said they were busy laying track clear across the prairie to San Francisco and the endless ocean? Oh, Charlie, Charlie.

Hillsdale was the next stop. Then, with a change, Jonesville, and she would make sense of her father's letter. Becca dared not pray for either boy meanwhile, lest the price of one life be that of the other. She was not optimistic. When she was a child, things had turned out nicely as a rule. Now she expected things to turn out for the worst, and they usually did. At Hillsdale the connecting train was late. The sun had set before Becca reached Jonesville, and the night was lit only by lightning.

# FIFTEEN

## *The Quick and the Dead*

AFTER WAITING A FEW MINUTES at the deserted depot Becca concluded that the telegram Tunis was to send to her parents had either not been sent or was undelivered. She would have to leave the trunk until morning, but, strong for her size, Becca thought nothing of lugging her hatbox and bulging carpetbag a quarter mile to the Clarendon House. For the first time, it crossed her mind that she might arrive home only to find strangers in residence. Franklin Case, Sr., had proved no more successful as an innkeeper than he had as a farmer. Horses were his trade, though he never quite had his son-in-law Carll Burr's touch with them.

"Hasn't been such a welcome since Lafayette toured the states," Becca muttered to herself as she gloomily trudged up a blackened Main Street. Only the undertaker's blazed with light. A crowd spilled forth into the street.

She wondered who had died, but did not dare ask, suffering dire visions only to overhear at last that it had been old Granny Keitel, one of the settlers, as the few survivors of Jonesville's first years were called. Granny Keitel who sat rocking on her porch, screeching at passing schoolchildren, "Why are you

146

smiling? What's there to smile about?" Becca had made a point of always walking on the far side of the street there. She would not miss the departed, but setting down her burden beyond the last reassuring lights of town, the premonition lingered; a funeral had attended her homecoming.

Becca could see the Clarendon House a long way off, a dark silhouette on the slope. A lamp burned in the kitchen window. Tiptoeing up to the glass, she was relieved to see her mother sitting before the stove, stringing apple rounds against the winter to come.

"Becca?" her mother exclaimed, half rising as Becca pushed open the door with her carpetbag. "Rebecca, you scared the life out of me. What are you doing here at this hour?" Quickly her astonishment gave way to pleasure, and she embraced her daughter. "I had no idea you were coming."

The two women stood back, appraising each other. "You've gained considerable weight, daughter," her mother observed.

"And you've lost, Ma," Becca said, remembering her father's letter. "Pa here?"

"There's the trotting meet over to Hillsdale," her mother explained. "George and Theodore are here, but they're both asleep." She nodded toward the stairs. "All right, tell me, Rebecca."

"Tell you what, Ma?"

"Why you're home. You look worried."

"I didn't say that, Ma."

"I know, but you've got worries and you're asking yourself, do I tell Ma, or don't I?"

Becca hesitated, then laughed in a halfhearted way. "Is there any coffee left, Ma?" As her mother poured her a cup, she said, "I can't fool you, can I? Pa wrote me, you know. Which one is home?"

"Which one?" Her mother seemed confused as she turned

from the stove. "Oh, you mean Alex. Alex is home. His sister went and fetched him clear from Washington City. Didn't you know?"

"How could I?" Becca sat down heavily, spilling some of the coffee. "How is he?"

"Doing just fine. Have no fear for our Alex."

"That the truth, Ma?"

"Have I ever lied to you, daughter?"

"Thank God for that," Becca exclaimed, and because her mother frowned, she apologized for using the Lord's name.

"It's not to me you should apologize," her mother admonished, which caused Becca not to think of the deity, but of Charlie. By celebrating Alex's life, was she somehow accepting doom for his friend?

Becca cleared her throat nervously. "Ma, do you know anything about Charlie Gregory?" she asked apprehensively.

"Simply that he's gone missing," her mother replied, her voice suggesting the Gregory boy was up to his old tricks. "Missing, and presumed dead," pronouncing the last bit like a judicial sentence.

"Dear God"—that word again—"and I knew it all the while."

"See here, Rebecca, it's not the end of the world." Her mother held her tight, her hands patted Becca's back, and she made the soothing noises Becca remembered from her childhood.

"I just want to die."

Her mother gave her a final tight squeeze of reassurance. "I'll pour us another cup of coffee, and then we'll both of us be off to bed." Becca's mother could scarcely write her own name, but she always said the right thing.

They sipped the coffee in silence. Becca was exhausted, her mother unwell. Both of them sat slumped before the stove until Sarah stood up painfully, observing, "Sometimes I'm a nasty-tempered old thing."

Becca felt obliged to deny this. They did not argue. She followed her mother up the creaking stairs as though she climbed a scaffold. Her old room looked strange somehow, smaller than she remembered. Her body craved sleep, but for a long time she lay awake, thinking. She made not a sound in the silent building, but tears ran down her face, unheeded. Of course Charlie was never meant for settling down, for children, for making a nest. She would marry by and by, when the war was done, and she would be a good and steadfast wife, never letting on that her husband had wed something that belonged in part to the wind that blew from the West, and that she would always feel the caresses of that breeze on her hair.

When Becca finally slept, she slept hard. A dazzle of sun aroused her, along with the sounds of her mother belaboring the pots and pans and her two younger brothers arguing as usual. "I must visit Alex today," she said as she sat, still exhausted, on the edge of the bed. "I must try to look pretty." The slanted mirror above the dresser had a faint coating of dust on its surface. Fine; it made her look the way she felt. She set about transforming herself from near-hag into beauty, sucking a piece of sugar filched the night before from the kitchen. It was her grandmother's remedy for curing gloom, and it gave her the energy to wash and dress. She went downstairs as flounced and pretty as she could make herself, apprehensive about looking Alex in the face; not because of what she might see, but because of what he might discern behind her rice powder.

After greeting her younger brothers in the stable, she went on to the Forman place. Alex's mother motioned Becca toward the stairs, excusing herself for not coming with her. The older woman's cough seemed to rack her heavy body. To Becca's surprise, Alex was sitting in a chair. He tried to rise, grimaced, and fell back. "You shouldn't have returned on my account," he said.

"Of course I should," she replied, kissing his forehead.

"It's the same place again," he gestured toward his leg. "Crazy, isn't it?"

"Well, you look like a million dollars," Becca informed him, and in fact, he did look surprisingly well. She would never admit there was more to her hasty journey home.

"Confederate dollars, I'll bet," and more seriously, "I guess I owe you a visit to New York one of these days." She was silent, and he went on, "This time the bullet went in and out clean as a whistle. I was lucky. I'll be up and around in no time, back with the old Seventh before you can shake a stick."

The last barrier to her reticence dissolved, and Becca said fiercely, "Don't you dare! I'll shake more than a stick if you try that, Alex Forman. Not if this war lasts a hundred years."

"Becca, it's all right," he protested. "I'm mustered out. Honest."

"For good?" she asked, suspicious.

"Well, for now at least. We'll see."

They were both silent again. At last Alex said, "I'll probably always have a limp."

"That doesn't matter, Alex." Another silence. She cleared her throat nervously. "Alex, can we talk about Charlie?"

He looked down at his hands. "If you like."

"But you'd rather not?"

"Just so long as I have an excuse to look at you," he said, half smiling.

She looked away, stared out the window. "Alex, I only want to know what happened." Her hands were beginning to tremble, and she hid them in the folds of her skirt.

Alex shook his head. "I don't know. I wish I did."

"But you were there," she protested, turning to him. "You pledged to stick together, you two."

"We did, Becca, the first day. Then on the second . . . There was so much confusion. . . . I called to him. I did, Becca. I kept on calling."

"I know you did," she said, suddenly contrite. "It's not your fault, Alex. I know that."

"But it may be, Bec." He'd never called her that before. "I keep thinking, it's my fault. If only we hadn't become separated . . ."

The next words were hard to say, and she rehearsed them in her mind. "Is Charlie dead, then, for certain?"

"Officially. Well, I suppose, yes."

But who could kill Charlie Gregory? Yet perhaps, she thought, that aura of immortality was only a kind of final doom that he had all along accepted, neither seeking nor fleeing from it. Surely Charlie Gregory would succumb to no stray or incidental bullet. If one took his life, who could doubt its purpose?

"Alex, did you . . ." Becca hesitated, doubting her mouth could ask such a question. "I have to speak plainly, even if it sounds awful. Alex, did you see his body?"

"Bec, oh, Bec!" There it was again, Charlie's name for her. "When somebody's reported missing, sometimes it's a question of . . . well, identification. You see, after a battle, sometimes the, ah, the bodies lie around for days, and in the hot weather, well, they change. And sometimes if you're fighting from behind a barricade, like we were, with only your head sticking out—"

"That's enough." Becca stopped the recitation. She had never been able to believe that when a person died they were just nothing. They had to be somewhere, and Charlie had such an inexhaustible sense of motion and embroilment. She still had hopes of seeing him return, eager and lighthearted, tanned, with all the South in his face.

"I know, Becca. It's hard for me, too," Alex said. He put his hand over hers, and the knuckles beneath his palm felt like a frail backbone that had been broken. "It's hard for me too, Bec, losing old Charlie."

Without knowing why she did so, Becca drew Alex's hand up to her throat. "Now say his name."

"Charlie Gregory," he said, and he felt her pulse surge up and let his hand fall away.

"Was that cruel?" she said with real concern. "I didn't mean it to be. It's just the way I am, deep down. Up here"— she touched her forehead—"it's always been you, Alex. I'm sorry."

"I know, Becca. Don't you suppose I always have?"

Through pain and suffering, Alex had learned humility, and through surviving, he had discovered a measure of self-confidence and pride. He could compete with the dead as honorably as he always had with the living. "I almost forgot," he said, "there's a present for you." Leaning on crutches and despite Becca's protestations, Alex lurched to the dresser and fumbled in a top drawer. "For you," as he pressed a small parcel into her hands.

"For me?"

"Charlie left it with me that last day, just in case."

So it was that Becca unwrapped the two gold nuggets fashioned into earrings.

"I believe he had them shipped from San Francisco," Alex said. Tears ran down his cheeks. For a moment he must have seen himself reflected in Becca's eyes. "Don't cry, Bec."

"You're the one who's crying. Who said I'm crying? I'm not."

Alex touched a finger to her cheek. "What's this, then?" He shed tears still, no longer for his lost friend, but for her loss, generous tears that Alex had spent on no other person.

"What shall we do?" she asked, and at last met his eyes.

"I don't know," he admitted.

"If you don't know, Alex, how am I to ever know?"

Presently Becca went for a walk. She made it a long and solitary one, a time for thought, from which came a single resolution. She had always deemed her ears too large for emphasis, but now she would get her ears pierced. She would wear Charlie's earrings and never take them off.

# SIXTEEN

## A Long-Distance Courtship

ALEX WAS RECOVERING FROM HIS WOUND almost too quickly for Becca. She feared, against all her protests, that he might reenlist, and when he took the train for Detroit she was frantic. "I was terrified," she admitted upon his return. "I was sure you'd join up again."

"Hardly that, Becca," he explained, pleased by her concern. "In fact, it's quite the contrary," and he showed her his official mustering-out document.

To All Whom It May Concern

Know ye that Alexander A. Forman, a corporal of Captain Henry Baxter's Company (C) Seventh Regiment of Mich. Infantry who was enrolled on the nineteenth day of June one thousand eight hundred and sixty-one to serve three years or during war, is hereby discharged from the service of the United States, this Seventh day of November 1863 at Detroit Barracks Mich. by reason of a gun shot wound on the inner side of right thigh near the knee impairing the free use of the joint. He is one-fourth disabled. Said Alexander A. Forman was born in Scipio, Michigan, Hillsdale Co., in the State of Michigan, is twenty-one years of age, five feet ten inches high, dark complexion, Hazel eyes, Brown hair, and by occupation, when enrolled, a Student.

Given at Detroit Barracks this Tenth day of November 1863
By order of Lt. Col. Smith
Military commander

This stilled her fears that Alex might elect to throw his life away, but there remained the spectre of the draft. Volunteering had lost its appeal, and despite the fearful riots in New York, the federal government needed men. Some communities, like Allen's Prairie, raised money to provide a bounty to keep their men at home, but Hillsdale had a war meeting, with bells ringing to bring out volunteers, and those who gained exemptions because of war injuries or other disabilities were featured in the local newspaper's "Coward List."

"Even if you're on that horrid list, you can't let that bother you. Alex, are you listening?"

"Absolutely, Bec." Alex loved how, when she was enthusiastic or excited, her mouth had a way of working in different directions.

"Alex, stop laughing. It's not funny." Becca was indignant.

"Well, you're funny sometimes. So fierce."

"What about Little Sturgeon?" Becca asked, fierce as she could be. She knew Alex had an offer from Mr. Gardiner to help open a lumber mill and associated store on Wisconsin's Sturgeon Bay. On the map, it looked like the end of the world, far beyond the reach of the draft, and she urged him to go.

"I believe you want to get rid of me," he chided.

"You know better than that, Alex. It's a future, a safe one, for now, anyway."

With the Gardiners, an ambitious young man could go far. Among their spreading ventures was the Jonesville woolen mill, making cloth for army uniforms. A good many of Becca's girlfriends now worked there, and but for her mother's frail health, she too might have become a factory worker, a prospect that Becca did not enjoy, though with her father's improvidence, the family could certainly use the money.

Alex's trip was briefly delayed when his mother fell ill. Upon her improvement late that autumn, he left, though he still did not look fit for a frontier adventure. Gallant as always, Alex would not let Becca carry his bag even part of the way to the depot, though she could tell by the hang of his coat and trousers that he had lost considerable weight. His left leg seemed to drag a bit, and he humped his shoulder as he climbed aboard the train, then gazed out through the car's dirty window with such a long, lonely, loving, wistful stare that Becca's toes tried to curl up inside her shoes.

This separation began their long courtship by letter, a time of change and adventure for both, as the Cases finally did move northwest again, to the hamlet of Pulaski on the axed fringe of the still-wooded wilderness. A good brooming and whitewashing and a change of name from the Haynes Tavern to the Pulaski House did not make the establishment a moneymaker nor Franklin Case a successful manager. Pulaski simply lacked the population to support such a facility, and after the first slow month, Pa turned back to his trotters. Becca, with only her mother, younger brothers, occasionally Douglas and a morose Julia for companionship, never accepted the place. She confided to her journal, "If I live here long, methinks I shall die of the blues."

Meanwhile, Alex was writing his first letter from Wisconsin.

Becca, I must tell you of my trip up here. The train of course was uneventful but in Chicago I found the steamer was laid up and I was obliged to ship aboard the two-masted schooner "Challenger". Believe me, with a northwester blowing, the high seas off Virginia were quickly forgotten and I must have seemed a green and sickly specimen to Jimmy Gardiner when he met me at the wharf. Little Sturgeon is nearly surrounded by a beautiful bay, where wild duck and fish are plentiful. A large grist mill and saw mill go together with a boarding house and store, quite a number of inferior buildings and four or five large houses, ninety voters, farming, wild game, blackberries, cranberries. Jimmy has a sailboat and I saw deer swimming in the lake.

Indians still fished there with nets and held their feasts in the clearing on the Saint Marys River. Part of Alex's job as purchasing agent for the Gardiners was to supply the Indians with iron kettles in exchange for blackberries to be made into jam for the growing cities on the lower lakes. A canal with two locks had already been dug around the rapids on the Saint Marys River, and ore steamers used them while the furnaces on the lower lakes left a spreading haze of blue smoke that spoke of changing times.

Alex's letters were full of excitement, but Becca, who once again yearned for New York, did not love Pulaski, where she watched her mother's uncertain health with concern and sometimes lay awake over her sister-in-law Julia, who seemed morbidly convinced that she could not survive the birth of another child. For release, Becca rode the old gray into a lather, never mentioning her horsemanship to Alex, who thought her reckless.

Alex hinted at engagement. Becca wrote back that she dared not trust her heart until peace returned. Charlie's name was never mentioned, but with Christmas coming, Alex punished her with:

I have written my parents concerning my once more enlisting under the "old stars and stripes" and shall see how they feel this time before I go.

By return mail Becca wrote:

> I never want to hear that U.S.A. is again attached to your name and am fearful that I shall. You may not think me very brave. Once I would have said, "Yes, go," but no longer. I think so differently about the war than I used to altho' the federal army now seems to meet success on every hand. I cannot make it seem that Charlie G. is dead. . . .

This was one of the few mentions of Charlie in her letters, but it was a season when veterans were responding to the four-hundred-dollar bounty being offered by the government, or simply to pride, for if numbers were not kept up, the old regiments were absorbed into new ones.

Happily for Becca, Alex seemed to demonstrate a change of heart when he replied:

> Becca, I can not call you unpatriotic for I too, share your feelings in reference to once more enlisting under my Country's banner. I have suffered willingly, and would have lain down my life if necessary, but not just now with the war going so well.

Relieved, Becca told him of holiday preparations, the making of pies, proposed sleighing parties, in the hopes Alex might visit for a few days. But winter was hard in the north, with transportation from Little Sturgeon often cut off now that the lakes were frozen. Christmas Eve found Becca and her mother up late making new dolls. She wrote Alex about how some friends had gone into the woods looking for vines to make hoop skirts, returning with poison ivy vines and almost perishing of the itch.

Christmas came and went. Ice broke on the lakes. General Grant had taken over in the east and expounded his rule of war: "Find out where your enemy is, get at him as soon as you can, strike him as hard as you can, and keep moving on."

On April 14 her sister Sarah wrote Becca about the big parade of colored regiments that marched past their Brooklyn house. With *US* stamped on their belt buckles, there'd be no return to slavery. "I am sure Charlie would be pleased," Becca commented in her journal.

Presently Grant and Lee were slugging it out, day after flaming day in Virginia's wilderness. News came that General Baxter, former colonel of the Seventh Michigan, had been wounded in the leg. He returned to duty, only to receive a shoulder wound.

While home, Baxter had turned the Pulaski House's long ballroom into an enlistment center. With a bounty of 150 dollars, Becca's brother Douglas enlisted, despite Julia's impassioned tears.

"I'll never see you alive again," she pleaded. Douglas looked sad, yet he went. "I believe he wants a breather from wife and children," Becca wrote. "I could use one myself," though she would not have wanted Cold Harbor as the alternative.

There Grant, having sent forward wave after wave of men in hopeless assault, was given the nickname "Butcher," but he never considered retreat. Instead he slipped around the Confederate flank, came close to taking Petersburg, the key to the capital, and failing this, initiated the long bloodletting siege that would continue the better part of a year. Throughout this campaign, the dwindling Seventh Michigan was involved.

In the west, Sherman backed General Johnston's Confederates up against Atlanta, with the Union pickets yelling, "How many of you are there left, Johnny?" to receive the reply, "Oh, about enough for another killing." And so the war went on, with nearly balanced and corresponding weapons, the opponents like two insects ready to fight on to the death.

At this point, Franklin Case was having second thoughts about Pulaski. His last generous guest list was in September, when Becca wrote, "The thrashers were here to breakfast, dinner, and supper, only ten of them." But young men were hard to find even for the harvest, and when this lot moved on to other fields, the hotel was quiet enough for Becca to renew her horseback riding. She made frequent trips to Jonesville, sufficient to practice what she considered a secret vice, one she only hinted at even in her diary. Becca became a train watcher. She knew hope might never alter tomorrow's weather, but still Becca searched the arriving passengers, the limping veterans of Sherman's western army, the wounded returning from Petersburg, seldom seeing anyone she knew, and never Charlie Gregory. All she wanted at the time was Charlie alive somehow.

There were ghosts about her, the memories of boys she had known who had gone off, clutching their guns, to kill or be killed because they dared not be cowards. Once she had heard a voice on the train platform singing clear and in tune, the words barely intelligible, but with a gasp of recognition she had run, run to the voice with a pounding heart, only to confront a stranger with a bandage where his nose ought to be, and she'd wanted to ask, Doesn't it hurt to sing that way?

But the veteran had tried to smile, and she'd said only, "It's good to have you home again."

But no, it wasn't Charlie, never Charlie, though Jonesville was clearly haunted by the shades of soldiers who would not be returning. Gradually Becca gave up the practice, and in her diary she speculated, was there a pattern to life? Since her days in Sunday school, she had believed that life had purpose and meaning, but what if all was accidental, life and death purely chance? This was not a question Becca could confront for long.

Toward the end of August 1864, Becca attended a barn dance. Two fiddles played until midnight, whereupon she and her friends took the long, giggling ride home in a hay wagon. She recounted all this to Alex in what may have been an effort to elicit jealousy. His reply, with uncommon subtlety, ignored the bait and chose instead to celebrate two glorious Union victories, Admiral Farragut's in Mobile Bay and Sherman's seizure of Atlanta. Then he referred to a growing fire of patriotism in his bosom, a clear hint of possible reenlistment.

Becca ignored these tactics, and described her part in Jonesville's autumn fair, which raised 400 dollars for soldiers' aid. By this time, Jonesville's draft quota had been filled.

A presidential election was upcoming, and though Becca had no vote, she was closer to the excitement than Alex, since her father's present hotel had been a recruiting center before and was a polling station now, and if unruly drunks had to be escorted to the door, Franklin Case was the man for the job.

Former general McClellan ran as a Democrat in opposition to President Lincoln, and though he did not renounce the war, many of his supporters were avowed Copperheads who declared the war a failure thus dooming McClellan's cause since the war was suddenly going well. Few loved the "little Napoléon" as before. Alex wrote in outrage:

When I think of the cowardly and traitorous class of men called "Peace Democrats" who are lying in wait "like foxes for their prey" ready to throw every obstacle in the way of success to our glorious cause, my heart almost rises to my throat with indignation.

On November 5 he added:

I plan to cast my first vote for Lincoln, Liberty and Union.

On October 30 Becca took note of a cornhusking at the Pulaski Hotel. She and her mother baked cakes and her father brought in plenty of apples and cider. November 8 was recorded as another long, tiresome day, as voters came to cast their ballots. The village went solidly for Lincoln, as did the nation.

Within the week, General Sherman had begun his march from Atlanta, which would cut a flaming wound through the heart of Dixie, to the sea. There was a monstrous logic in this mission: to destroy the Southern economy and hope, with dusty blue columns burning much that required burning, putting a final torch to slavery and the old plantation way of life, consuming the grand and gracious with terrible fires that all the same lit the way to a more humane future that had to be.

One General Cleburne suggested that the Confederate army recruit black slaves with the promise of freedom, but the notion was treated as an obscenity in polite society. Meanwhile in Michigan, Becca saw Alex's name in the paper and wrote to him, but without her former alarm.

I saw your name in the list of candidates for the next draft which I don't think will ever come off.

In response, Alex fought back with:

> I have been tempted with a lieutenancy in a Wisconsin regiment from this county. Shall I go? Me thinks you might take a more reasonable hour to return from picnics than midnight. I am fearful.

On Friday, November 18, 1864, Becca entered in her diary, "President Lincoln has declared the last Thursday of this month a national day of Thanksgiving. It is said that when he is no longer President he will take the cars west to California. How like poor Charlie. Mr. Buck, the photographer, has sold out and left town. I purchased of the artist the last picture of my dear friend."

Becca thought a good deal about Charlie that autumn, and told her diary on Christmas day, "A merry Christmas had here. Ma came down and said she felt much better. We emptied our stockings before breakfast. I received from Sarah and Tunis a beautiful new-style black beaver hat with gay strings. We were all well remembered. How short a time it seems since two years ago. Charlie Gregory was at our house more than once that day. He is now gone from this earthly home forever tho' he died honorably. How little we know if another Merry Christmas will greet us here again. Life is uncertain, and I wish I were a better girl. I wore Charlie's earrings again today. But for Ma's disapproval I would wear them always."

Alex wrote from Little Sturgeon of more austere celebrations:

> Mr. Mansfield is here and there is preaching every night. On Christmas there were four ducked under the ice and kept there until their sins were forgiven.

When Becca wrote longingly of New York and its distractions, Alex replied soberly:

> You have been thrown in different society of late and plainly perceive the difference. I once thought our tastes were very near alike, but I fear 'tis not so. Give me the comforts of a quiet home when duty is lain aside, where love and confidence reign supreme and I ask not for the formal pleasures of society.

At this point he was teaching Sunday School on a weekly basis. The Cases, on the other hand, were planning a holiday dance at the hotel, with Franklin swearing that if it wasn't a success, he would sell the place.

"Hardly anyone attended our dance," Becca recorded. "Perhaps it was the snow." Then turning to the subject of Alex, she added, "Sometimes I find AA a little stuffy." But how could she ignore his last lines?

> Oh would that I could fly to your side this Sabbath eve and remain there til we could have a long talk.

With the war winding down, they were falling in love from sheer relief, and almost without being aware of the process. They had known each other for years, had had moments when love awakened, but had tended for the most part to take each other for granted. Certainly Becca had avoided involvement. Why complicate things? Why speak of love? For a while they beat around the word, until Alex began using it with unremitting insistence, as he had used the threat of reenlistment. At last Becca capitulated with:

> Alex, I tell you solemnly, I love you with all the heart that's left in me.

No more was needed. Love produced a desire to be loved; desire to be loved spawned a conviction of being loved. Around and around they went until Alex concluded:

I cannot help feeling that there is a bright future in store for us, Bec, and hope we are not counting too much on earthly happiness, for Providence will cause us to enjoy it as he wills.

Further development of their romantic thoughts were interrupted by a tragedy. Alex's mother had been ailing all winter with a congestion in her lungs, and she died despite the doctor's best efforts. Alex received his father's terse letter and arrived home from Little Sturgeon too late for the funeral. She was buried in the Jonesville cemetery beside Alex's two older sisters, who had died in childhood. Alex returned to Little Sturgeon only weeks before his father's hasty remarriage. It was a marriage Alex could neither condone nor forgive.

By April his spirits had lifted considerably, and on the fifth he wrote to Becca:

Can't you come up and help me a little? O, what glorious news we are receiving from our armies. The people here would not believe it the first days the news came and consequently did not celebrate until last evening and then we had a glorious time. Bonfires, cannon, martial music, speaking, singing and I wish you could have been here. It was a wonderful evening and everything and everybody seemed to rejoice. The clouds are beginning to break from our political horizon and peace, bright peace, a thousand times welcomed seems about to burst forth from its fettered chains.

But the dying Confederacy clung to life, and on April 12 Alex added:

But seriously Becca, it will be a glorious day of Jubilee all over the land when victory is achieved. May a just God grant it before long.

Becca, ever the teetotaler, replied:

Yes, Alex, one of these days I may just pay you a surprise visit and though I agree victory may warrant a celebration, I trust I shall not hear of you in a pitiable condition. An honorable wound is one thing but I cannot promise to take care of one who has "spreed it." By the way, did you hear, Brother Frank has been promoted captain. I am glad to believe that the Fifteenth Michigan is unlikely to see further battle.

Meanwhile, General Lee, the aristocratic spokesman of the old South, sat down with General Grant, the midwestern businessman and representative of America's unshaven future, at Appomattox Courthouse for the surrender of the Army of Northern Virginia. Clearly Alex saw the sadness behind the joy of victory when he wrote:

For the first time I felt sorry for the brave fellows. If their cause is not just, they have been true to it and it must be like death itself for a brave fighter to lay down his arms before his enemy.

Before this letter could arrive, Becca was writing in her diary, "Pleasant weather. Father went to the station this morning and took my letter but with what horrible news he returned, the murder of our noble president Abraham Lincoln at Fords theatre Thursday evening by an individual supposed to be an actor named J. W. Booth. Nothing Shakespeare ever wrote could hardly compare with the tragic air of this murder before a large audience in the theatre. Our rejoicing this week has been unbounded but it has terminated with the greatest cause for mourning our country can possibly know."

This news found Alex in Chicago while the presidential funeral train was in the station, and he wrote:

> I passed in with the crowd and viewed the remains of our beloved President and never shall forget the sight, so solemn and impressive. You have read of the richness and grandeur of the catafalco wherein were deposited the honored remains, escorted by thirty-six maidens clad in white, one for each state of our restored Union. Becca, it was majestic.

Moved by similar instincts, Becca made the trip into Jonesville for a memorial service, writing in her diary: "Tuesday, April 19, 1865, Rainy, cloudy day. How sad the town looked, all deeply draped in mourning for the honored dead. Every private house has the windows craped, with more black material looped around the front doors. At the Presbyterian church we heard Mr. Childs. His language was excellent but he lacks the power of good delivery. The church presented a very solemn aspect, so draped in mourning, and it seemed as if the day was just appropriate to the sad occasion."

From Philadelphia she received a letter from an old Brooklyn schoolmate recounting the hysteria of her neighbor, the assassin Booth's sister, upon learning of her brother's deed.

On June 26 Becca's sister-in-law Julia died in childbirth. Becca washed and laid out her body for burial. "We have today attended the funeral of Julia," Becca wrote in her journal. "Poor girl, she was a constant sufferer but she rests now though the cold rain is falling on her grave tonight. We expected this and yet as is always the case it seemed very sudden and impossible to realize. Such a short time before her death she was talking so gaily with mother and I while Douglas was feeding her strawberries. She has left three motherless children, another little girl now named Julia."

Though Douglas had been discharged from the army with her other brothers, Frank with the rank of captain, the care of the three motherless children fell largely to Becca and her mother. Becca found them tiring but rewarding. When time permitted, she rode her father's new pony, telling her journal afterward that she was almost too stiff to walk and that she had been obliged to get up throughout the night with the colicky baby, whom she loved dearly. Yet, Becca wrote in her diary, "Julia was so silent and gloomy when alive that it is hard to miss her now that she is gone."

Julia's death seemed to strengthen certain ties, and Becca could write to Alex the nice things her parents were now saying about him, to which Alex replied:

I am reassured to be told that I am held in high esteem by both your parents. I once thought your father preferred Charlie G.

Such circumstances seemed to spur their courtship. Alex wrote boldly:

Becca, I feel like having a real frank talk with you tonight and am going to do so. I look forward with bright anticipation to the time when I may have the right to cherish and protect you through life and hope and pray it may not be far ahead in the dim future.

This prompted a blushing Becca to confide in her diary. "Saturday, October 21st, 1865. Pleasant. This afternoon took a walk to the P.O. and was rewarded by receiving my expected epistle from Dearest Alex. He writes, 'I have a faint idea of making a permanent arrangement on my next visit to you' and also 'how will such an arrangement suit Becca?' I must be confiding with someone, journal, and you are the best one I know. To be addressed thus by him seems new and strange. I knew that someday we would talk of marriage and I have long anticipated it, yet both of us have been very silent on this topic. It seems as if we must have been too much so, for to talk of it now seems like a frank answer to all his questions and the dear fellow shall receive frankness from me. I think it is time now to throw off so much of this long existing reserve and share each other's thoughts and feelings. I do anticipate much happiness with my best loved one, and feel as if in loving so well, I am loved in return."

Julia's death was the last straw for Becca's father. The Pulaski House went promptly on the market, and the Cases soon moved, not back to Jonesville as Becca hoped, but north to the rapidly growing city of Jackson. Presently she received word that Alex was returning to go into business with his father. She rode into Jonesville to meet that train for which she had so often searched before in vain.

On the platform Alex paused and felt the wind in his collar. Leaning on his stick, he gazed around at the Michigan autumn, then limped past the depot, raising one shoulder slightly higher than the other. His wounds had healed into scars. They would be with him always. He was just glad to be alive. Yet why did the November wind seem so cold?

Then a slight, brown-haired girl with a trim figure came walking in a strangely elderly way, leaning forward as she moved. It was Becca, who had been disappointed by so many arriving trains, but when she saw Alex she cried out and began to run, and the motion transformed her into a girl again. "Bec!" he exclaimed. "You did come!" as they embraced.

"Don't look at me," she said. "I've cried so long my face is swollen."

"I don't care. I love you so much," he whispered.

"Say it again," she whispered back.

Then brightening, holding her chin up with his fingers, "As often as you like. I love saying it, Becca. I love you. I love you."

"It's a lovely word," she agreed.

"Then don't cry anymore."

As they walked through Jonesville, Alex said, "I heard they plan to put up a monument to Charlie and the others."

"What on earth for? All he did was die," she said. The war seemed long ago, its purpose lost in time.

"I think he died for men's freedom," Alex replied. "There are worse things to die for."

"I know," Becca acknowledged, resenting herself for resenting all those who had given up their lives.

"And just because they never came back, we still owe them something."

"Yes, I suppose, a statue for remembrance," Becca agreed, but statues were so cold. She sank her head onto Alex's shoulder, her eyes fixed on some hazy future, thinking, There are things I ought to say, but if he kisses me again, I never will. And Alex did kiss her, repeatedly: her lips, her forehead, her hair, until Becca was breathless, while murmuring, "I know, Bec, I know." And he did know. There was no need to speak of Charlie again, for Alex knew and accepted all, and it was enough that they were alive and together, for the future was always a miracle.

# SEVENTEEN

---

## *Happily Ever After*

ALEX'S WIDOWED FATHER had, with unseemly haste it seemed to Becca, first married a mysterious Mrs. Tubbs and then opened a general store in nearby Burr Oaks, with the inducement to Alex that it be called Forman and Son. But perhaps Becca disapproved of James Forman's remarriage more in principle than in fact, for her only comment on the second Mrs. Forman after meeting her on the street was, "She is a real lively little woman and quite a tease."

Burr Oaks and Jackson were sufficiently removed so as to keep Becca and Alex's courtship very much on paper. In December of 1865 a big fire in Burr Oaks's tiny commercial district nearly finished off the Forman enterprise. Most of the stock was saved, though; insurance covered the rest.

With the store again secure, Alex felt in a position to press marriage in concrete terms. For a time the issue was whether Alex should speak to Becca's parents in person or do so by way of a letter. He preferred the letter. She favored a meeting face to face and wrote encouragingly:

I have every reason to believe that my parents value my Alex as much as either of my two big brothers, and even now I often laugh when thinking how you used to tell me that Mother did not like you, but preferred Charlie.

On February 19, 1866, Alex had his way, writing from Burr Oaks to Becca's parents:

I have the blessed assurance from Becca's lips, that my deep, abiding love for her is returned, and it is to have your blessing and consent to our Union, in some future day, that I address you these lines. I am well aware of the trust I ask you to place in my hands and to cherish and protect her through this life and prove myself to you a Son worthy of your confidence and esteem will be my future aim and happiest task, in case you grant the boon I ask.

To this Franklin Case, Sr., responded with appropriate dignity:

Your letter of the 19th has been rec'd by myself and wife have pondered its contents. It will be a trial for us, especially a fond Mother to part with her last daughter, still we shall both of us give our cheerful consent and blessing and we hope that you may both long live to enjoy the happiness of a married life.

We know of no young man, whom we should more appreciate as a sun [sic] than yourself.

Now only the date remained at issue. "When?" Becca asked him, and Alex dutifully suggested the spring of 1867. Disturbed at the delay, Becca wrote back coyly, saying:

Please don't you go and leave me a hopeless Case.

172

This generated a rapid turnabout. Alex wrote:

If you will have me for better or for worse why not know your doom as soon as can be?

Becca now hesitated, considered consulting a fortune teller who arrived that spring with the circus, then thought better of it. "They charge a dollar or I should have had mine told but I thought it rather too steep, a dollar for just a little trash, all lies," she told her diary, then took the initiative and preferred an October date, the anniversary of the occasion when they had first mentioned marriage. "Too late," Alex countered, and it would be rather late in the year for a honeymoon, to which Becca very much looked forward, so a September date was finally chosen.

September could not arrive soon enough. For a honeymoon, she hinted at New York. Alex, who always favored the wilds, suggested Wisconsin. She had never visited the upper lakes, but they were not high on her list of places to go. "I should like very much to have my many good folks [in New York] know and doubtless approve my liege Lord," she replied temptingly. Alex seemed to relent, though he pointed out that "Cholera is fearfully on the increase there." Finally they compromised on Niagara Falls. After all, a marriage was hardly valid that did not include the Falls.

When the time came, they were married in the Case home in Jackson, Becca wearing her going-away dress of gray moire antique. Their solemn vows were followed by a bountiful reception in the flower-bedecked house.

The following day they were off by train, Buffalo bound. Becca sat in rapt contemplation before the window, trying to register everything of what would be her one-and-only honeymoon, when a wagon swept into view on a parallel road. Two boys and a girl rode behind the lathered horse, and as they passed, one of the lads stood up on the jostling seat and waved. "Charlie!" Becca never knew for sure whether she said the name aloud or whether it rang only inside her head. For a second, years were stripped away, then trees flashed by, erasing the vision from the window frame. The train chugged on through deep woods, and in that darkened mirror Becca peered through the glass at days departed. Why had he gone and died without letting her know? She would never see Charlie again, not if she lived for a million years. A great void seemed to open around her thoughts.

"Oh, Bec, Bec, look at you." It was Alex. "Look at you." Her eyes sparkled with unshed tears. "They say God made tears to be shed," he said, and put his arm around his bride, holding Becca close. "You can't grieve forever."

"I'm not grieving," Becca insisted. "I'm remembering." And the tears that welled up in her eyes were somehow happy tears, despite her sadness. "I am happy," she insisted, "I really am."

Then Alex chuckled. He was surprised to hear the dry sound emerge from his own lips. "Bec, believe me, my heart's in there with yours. You can tell me anything."

But she could never quite tell him. "I'm just being a silly," Becca replied. All that was gone. She was not the sort to relive the past or invent a might-have-been future. Always gone, never really dead, was Charlie, along with the innocent days before the war, and it wasn't worth writing any of this in her diary. Gone for the end of slavery. And yet, what were they to do with the freed negroes? Becca had no idea. No one else seemed to know. It was not material for her diary. No, she hardly knew what to tell her diary anymore.

They arrived before the thunderous flume of Niagara that

night and sat there enthralled, speechless. Alex seized hold
of his injured leg, as he always did when enraptured. He
observed finally, "Wouldn't old Charlie have loved this?" at
which Becca turned to her husband with, "Admit it, Alex,
you're glad we came."

That night she made the last regular entry in her diary.
"Tuesday evening, September 11, 1866, finds me sitting at a
round table with my Alex near me in a cosy nice sitting room
in the Frontier House at Niagara. Arrived here about 5 pm
and from that time (with the exception of just finishing supper)
we have been taking a splendid view of the great Niagara
Falls. They dressed us up in uniform to go down and see Table
Rock and also have a very close view of the Falls, i.e. to walk
under them a few steps. It was very rainy while going there
and has also been a dark cloudy day. The Falls, nature's work
and suspension bridge, the work of man exceeded my expecta-
tions. Alex is writing home and I am now going to do likewise."

Was it Charlie's wanderlust inside her that made Becca
yearn for new sights? Perhaps some of the same legacy in-
duced an expansive Alex to promise, "If it will make you
happy, we'll visit every state in the Union."

"I wish we could stop time," Becca replied. "That would
make me happy."

"Even a magician can't do that," he said. No, not even
God. "Time is something we have to use," and he confidently
expected that they would have their fair share of time together, and that they would use it well.

Alex was more right than he could realize. They were happy
and prospered in Michigan, just as happy and even more
prosperous when they moved back to Brooklyn, where Becca
became the good and devoted mother to four children, but
she was happiest returning to her journals when they traveled,
and Alex kept his word. They visited every state in the Union

at least once, then went abroad, while his scar turned from pink to blue to gray, in the end leaving but a small hollow above the knee marked by a silvery trace when the light struck it from a certain angle.

Becca renewed her diary on these frequent vacations, meticulously recording everything she saw of interest, but wherever they went, she never saw Charlie again, though Becca never entirely stopped looking. "Becca," she would tell herself, "you're a grandmother now, it's time to forget all that."

Forgetting was something that had to happen, but it never quite happened to her. Or to Alex. Charlie never entirely left either of them. He whispered in their ears now and then, shared their delights, put thoughts into their heads, made them smile and, sometimes, cry.

# EIGHTEEN

---

# *Afterward*

ALEX AND BECCA ARE NOW ONLY MEMORIES in the head of a granddaughter, herself a great-grandmother. She can tell you of Alex at eighty, a good-natured old man, rather stout and full of practical jokes, who liked to call her back as though it were an emergency, then pose the question, "Tell me, where would you have been now if I hadn't called you here?"

There is something that has been described as wisdom of the world, a sort of sixth sense giving balance during all of life's dislocations. It cannot be taught and takes years to attain. Alexander Forman seemed to have found it. In 1895 he was awarded the Congressional Medal of Honor for his conduct at Fair Oaks, and he received this honor with the bemused modesty with which he accepted all other good things. His granddaughter was far more impressed with the hollow in his left leg, made public on those long summer weekends after he had prospered in real estate and turned the business over to his own son, another Alexander, then moved to the south shore of Long Island. She remembers him best for his starring role on the Fourth of July. Alex never lost his abiding love for fireworks, and inevitably proposed, as the grandchildren hopped about eagerly, "What do you think, Bec? Just one more for old Charlie?" only to produce the most lethal sky-rocket they had ever seen.

With all their traveling, it was not until 1907 that Becca and Alex visited Virginia, by way of Willard's Hotel in Washington, D.C., and it was like old, old times when Becca sat down to her journal and wrote, "Monday, March 18th, a grand spring day. I have enjoyed it immensely. Soon after breakfast we started for Fair Oaks and Seven Pines, one of the awful battle-grounds of the civil war and where my precious hubby fought and bled for our great country. We first visited the national cemetery very close to the Fair Oaks station and registered, and an old veteran of Iowa, keeper of the grounds, guided us through the cemetery where 1388 soldiers were resting. Mr. Lyne, an old vet of the southern side lives close by and he furnished a two seated rig and took us all over the battle grounds, about eight miles. He has posted himself thoroughly and gave very correct truths of the war having lived in his old dilapidated house and neglected surrounds ever since the close of the war. He pointed out many ditches that the soldiers dug and more embankments that they threw up for their protection. The old farm house just back a few rods from the fight in which Alex and Charlie Gregory were engaged is still standing and Alex recognized it at once. So we drove the very field where my Soldier Boy fell in battle and I am so glad that though the wound was great and it took many months for him to recover and lay aside his crutches, that he is very much alive."

Alex and Becca never came to resemble each other, as two people often do who have been married for ages, and Becca's granddaughter recalls her as a humorless little old lady who smelled of camphor and who suspected her husband of cheating her at cards. They played pinochle incessantly during their later years, and he did cheat her unmercifully, though for all her accusations, Alex never did admit it. Old Becca often talked to herself, stirring up the heavy summer air with a black embroidered fan she had found on a trip to Spain. Her granddaughter remembered that the old lady wore her hair pulled back into a fierce knot on the back of her head, revealing enormous ears. "My father told me I had elfin blood, which means you do, too," she would explain, and her little granddaughter asked once, "And is that where those funny little earrings came from, the elves?" and Becca had thought, then replied, "Why, yes. I think we can say that." Those little gold earrings she wore until her death in 1928 at the age of 84. Alex, having died five years before, passed a gold pocket watch and his medal along to his namesake.

In all their travels, southern Pennsylvania was never considered, the field of Gettysburg never visited. After all, Charlie Gregory might have been encountered there, and neither Alex nor Becca would have known what to say to him after so many years. Their friend never did return after the war, never received a medal, though there remains among Becca's effects a tinted photograph of a boy in a blue kepi, Colt revolver in one hand, bowie knife in the other, a boy staring out in fierce amusement, his eyes very much alive from a moment all but faded into oblivion.

For a graveyard to become a real graveyard, many dead must rest there. Many curious feet must tread upon them. Generations must pass. It must have time to become a place that belongs to the departed. It must belong more to them than to the living, who enter only as occasional visitors. And so it was when the author trudged up Cemetery Hill above Gettysburg in the sultry dusk of June 30, 1990. Tiny, fluttering flags adorned every grave, for it was the eve of battle recalled. To the west, above the Alleghenies, a gathering storm rum-

179

bled, ghostly armies in collision once again. Charles W. Gregory lies there forever, steadfast among the young volunteers of Michigan's Seventh Regiment, Company C, Jonesville Light Guards, who marched away to see the elephant in the summer of 1861 and in their innocence died, while changing the world forever.